I0600435

Moving Mountains

by Lawrence Roman

A SAMUEL FRENCH ACTING EDITION

SAMUEL FRENCH

FOUNDED 1830

NEW YORK HOLLYWOOD LONDON TORONTO

SAMUELFRENCH.COM

ISBN 978-0-573-66331-4   Printed in U.S.A.   #9587

MUSIC USE NOTE

Licensees are solely responsible for obtaining formal written permission from copyright owners to use copyrighted music in the performance of this play and are strongly cautioned to do so. If no such permission is obtained by the licensee, then the licensee must use only original music that the licensee owns and controls. Licensees are solely responsible and liable for all music clearances and shall indemnify the copyright owners of the play and their licensing agent, Samuel French, Inc., against any costs, expenses, losses and liabilities arising from the use of music by licensees.

**IMPORTANT BILLING AND CREDIT
REQUIREMENTS**

All producers of *MOVING MOUNTAINS must* give credit to the Author of the Play in all programs distributed in connection with performances of the Play, and in all instances in which the title of the Play appears for the purposes of advertising, publicizing or otherwise exploiting the Play and/or a production. The name of the Author *must* appear on a separate line on which no other name appears, immediately following the title and *must* appear in size of type not less than fifty percent of the size of the title type.

CHARACTERS

GWEN – 58

CHARLIE FULLER – 67

ELAINE – Charlie's daughter, 36

POLLY ADAMSON – 62

ROBERT – Polly's son, 39

MARC – Polly's nephew, 34

HARRIET – 69

SETTING

The action takes place in Charlie Fuller's condominium in Santa Monica, California.

The time is the present. Summer.

ACT I

Scene One

(Charlie Fuller's condominium, part of a larger complex in Santa Monica, California, not far from the Pacific Ocean. This building goes back to the 1930s; the Spanish influence is clear. Rooms with high ceilings, archways, wooden beams. Through the passage of time, the apartment has been added to and possibly subtracted from, so it is very "free form" and hardly conventional in design.)

(The essentials are:)

(Bedroom, in an alcove, giving it a separateness from the rest of the living-dining-kitchen area. Off the bedroom, a door to the bathroom and another one into a sauna.)

(Office area for Charlie's desk, computer [with a distinctive red button], fax machine, addressograph machine, files, etc. Posters attest to Charlie's causes. SUPPORT GREENPEACE, NO SMOKING, NO NUKES.)

(Courtyard outside the apartment, seen through large arched window and glass door. Greenery. Possibly a fence and gate which leads to other condos which we do not see. Charlie's moped is visible. There is a front door leading to the street and a door, or archway, leading from kitchen to service porch in rear which we cannot see.)

(In decor, the apartment reflects the casualness of beach living. Also the colors of Charlie's life of which neatness is not one. Ethnic objects of art, books, record albums and many hanging plants to suck up the carbon dioxide.)

(AT RISE: The apartment is empty, or so it seems. All the blinds are down, blocking out the California summer

sun. The bed is mussed, a striped coverlet on it. If we looked closely, though at this point it is not imperative to see these things, a thick colored candle has burned low, a bottle of champagne is turned down in an ice bucket, the telephone is off the hook.)

(Quiet. So quiet. Then:)

*(**GWEN**, 58, attractive, somewhat matronly, with dyed red hair and a marvelous exuberance, bursts in from the bathroom singing "Zigeuner." A huge bath towel and nothing more covers her. But more importantly she feels wonderful and certainly doesn't mind letting it out. She does her version of a gypsy dance [the Noel Coward song] around the condo.)*

GWEN. Zigeuner!…Zigeuner!

(After a few wild flourishes, she stops, looks over at the bed which appears to be empty and:)

Charlie.

(no reply)

Charlie, are you alive?…Charlie, please do something to reassure me.

*(Now there is slow movement in the bed. **CHARLIE** is there. Unseen because his pajamas are of the same striped material as the coverlet)*

Charlie, what are you doing?

CHARLIE. Recovering.

(What we are witnessing is the aftermath of love in the afternoon.)

GWEN. Charlie, please, stand up and start breathing. Deeply so I can see that you still work.

CHARLIE. Watch!

(He bestirs himself, reassembles himself, reglues himself. Then he strikes a pose with:)

Zigeuner!

GWEN. *(joins in)* Zigeuner!

(Together they do their gypsy dance. Then, somewhat winded, they settle down, side by side, affectionately)

Yes, it's true, I guess. In a woman the fifties are the wicked years.

CHARLIE. If she's fortunate.

GWEN. Oh, Charlie, you're so wonderful to me. You're so patient.

CHARLIE. You may think it's patience, Gwen. I think I just react more slowly.

GWEN. Sometimes I think I'm so selfish. Do this, do that. Try this, try that. I ask so much. Funny, often I'm too embarrassed to ask "where's the bathroom?" With you I can ask anything. What pressure that must put on you.

CHARLIE. It is my privilege to help you expand your horizons.

GWEN. Are you sorry sometimes you got mixed up with me?

CHARLIE. What, and lose the 'chance to expand mine?

(They look at each other, smile.)

Zigeuner!

GWEN. Zigeuner!

(They're on their feet, doing their dance again. The door buzzer sounds.)

CHARLIE. Who the hell is that?

(He crosses to window, peeks out through the blinds.)

Damn it, it's my daughter!

(Alarm. And scurrying around.)

GWEN. I don't want her to see me here! I'll go out the back way!

CHARLIE. You can't, you're not dressed! Go into the bathroom!

GWEN. What if she has to go? Women always have to go!

CHARLIE. *(an idea)* The sauna!

    (GWEN darts for the sauna.)

Your clothes! Take your clothes!

    (Meanwhile, outside ELAINE has been pressing the door buzzer.)

ELAINE. Poppa, let me in! I know you're there! I saw you peek out! Poppa!

    (GWEN has snatched up her clothes, rushes into the sauna to hide. Now CHARLIE goes to the front door, opens it. ELAINE, his daughter, comes in. She dresses out of the Beverly Hills boutiques, carries a Saks Fifth Avenue carry-all.)

CHARLIE. *(as though he didn't know)* Oh, it's you.

ELAINE. Of course it's me. What took you so long? Poppa, it's two in the afternoon. You're still in your pajamas.

CHARLIE. *(annoyed)* Why don't you call when you're coming over? I told you, call when you're coming over. I've got a perfectly good phone.

    (He looks at the phone. It's off the hook, which ELAINE doesn't see.)

ELAINE. Which is always busy. Poppa, it's a beautiful day! Let some sunlight in!

    (opens the blinds)

There, that's better! So stuffy. Do you have something against fresh air?

    (throws open the glass door to the outside)

There!

    (Meanwhile, CHARLIE has surreptitiously put phone back on the hook. It rings immediately. ELAINE looks at the phone. CHARLIE makes no move to answer it. The answering machine goes on.)

CHARLIE'S VOICE. Charlie Fuller's place. Please speak.

FIONA'S VOICE. *(warmly)* It's Fiona, honey. Tuesday night's good with me. Let me know.

(Machine clicks off. **ELAINE** *is looking at* **CHARLIE**. *He explains.)*

CHARLIE. First Tuesday every month, Seniors' Investment Club. I usually drive her if she can go.

ELAINE. *(aware of messed-up bed)* Poppa, you've been in bed! You don't feel well!

CHARLIE. I feel fine!

ELAINE. Then what are you doing in bed in the middle of the day?!

CHARLIE. *(She can be so exasperating.)* It was there, I used it!

ELAINE. *(convinced)* You don't feel well!

(feels his forehead)

CHARLIE. I told you, I feel fine!

ELAINE. Stick your tongue out!

CHARLIE. Go have Bobby stick his tongue out! Stop treating me like an infant!

*(**ELAINE** sees the mess of dishes and pots in the kitchen area.)*

ELAINE. Look at that mess! Oh, Poppa, if Mom were alive she'd tear her hair out at you living like this!

CHARLIE. Leave Mom out of this! If Mom were here I wouldn't be living like this in the first place!
(wants her out) Now…

ELAINE. It's your arthritis.

CHARLIE. It's not my arthritis. I'm fine! Elaine, I walk every morning, I swim every afternoon. My blood pressure is 140s over 80s, my pulse is 70, my cholesterol is…

ELAINE. I still think you look funny. Poppa, go to George's office, let him examine you… Now I haven't much time, I'm having high tea with Marsha at the Beverly Wilshire. I want to see if this shirt fits you.

(She takes a shirt out of her carryall. It's a white dress shirt, long collar points, old-fashioned. **CHARLIE** *makes a sour face. He doesn't like it.)*

You said you need shirts.

CHARLIE. Yes, but not from the last century. I'll buy my own shirts.

ELAINE. You don't like it.

CHARLIE. *(though he doesn't)* I love it!

ELAINE. You don't have to love it if you don't like it.

CHARLIE. *(wants her out)* I love it, I love it, I like it, I like it!

ELAINE. Good! I bought you half a dozen.

> *(dumps the shirts on him)*

> Poppa, I'd like to stay and visit but I've got *a* million things to do.

CHARLIE. *(urging her toward door)* Another time.

ELAINE. We're redoing the kitchen, you know. I can't decide between Poggenpohl or Gaggeneau.

> *(has a list)* Let's see. I've got to drop George's check off at the broker, have his tuxedo pressed, get his racket restrung, did I tell you: George is buying a race horse?

CHARLIE. George is a very good doctor. Too bad he's not interested in medicine. Goodbye, Elaine.

ELAINE. Don't stay cooped up. It's a lovely day. Get out.

CHARLIE. Yes, yes, I will.

> *(has her out the open door)*

> *(Meanwhile,* **GWEN** *can't stand the heat in the sauna any longer. She pops out, wringing wet, gasping.)*

ELAINE. *(suddenly back in)* I better see if you have a fever. You look flushed.

> *(**GWEN** drops behind the bed.)*

> Where's your thermometer? I want to take your temperature. In the medicine chest.

> *(**ELAINE** goes into bathroom. **GWEN** stands up. **CHARLIE** sees her.)*

GWEN. *(hushed)* It's too hot in there! The heat's still on!

*(**CHARLIE** turns down dial, opens and shuts sauna door a number of times, trying to draw the heat out. **GWEN** pops back into sauna just as **ELAINE** appears, shaking down thermometer.)*

ELAINE. Here. Open.

CHARLIE. I'm not going to open!

*(But as he speaks, **ELAINE** puts thermometer in his mouth. In resignation, **CHARLIE** sits.)*

ELAINE. *(genuine concern for him)* Poppa, I don't know why you insist on living here like this by yourself. I told you, we'll fix up the apartment over the garage any way you like. We have a Home Entertainment Center. 42-inch TV, video games, soda fountain. I'll put in shuffleboard. You'll have things to do. Garden. Walk the dog. There'll always be someone around. You won't be alone. I worry about that at your age...

CHARLIE. *(takes thermometer out of mouth)* Any more of that age talk and I *will* get a fever. When will you understand that aging doesn't necessarily mean getting old?

(about thermometer)

Look! Absolutely normal! Now, please...

(wants her to go)

ELAINE. I still think you look pale.

CHARLIE. Before you said I looked flushed.

ELAINE. Maybe you need a tonic.

CHARLIE. I've got a tonic.

ELAINE. George'll prescribe something.

CHARLIE. It's already been prescribed. Elaine, *please*, I have to shower and leave. I'm meeting friends at the Center

(dig at her) for a red-hot game of dominos!

(She knows she has provoked him.)

ELAINE. Poppa, I'm concerned about you. I love you. I don't want anything to happen to you. I want you to be around to see the kids grow up.

CHARLIE. *(softens as she did)* Yes, dear, I know, but you shouldn't worry so much about me. I'm doing fine. Now go on, you've got a million things to do. I'll see you for Sunday dinner.

(She nods.)

My love to the kids. And to George too, even if he is a doctor.

*(**ELAINE** smiles, kisses him. She gives him the thermometer, goes. **GWEN** comes out of the sauna. She will dress through following.)*

GWEN. Charlie, if this keeps up I'm going to need a cooler hiding place.

CHARLIE. Are you all right?

GWEN. Marvelous! I just lost three pounds! Close call.

CHARLIE. Yes. I sometimes think I should hang a bell around her neck.

GWEN. Thank you for handling it. Not that I'm ashamed, but I really don't want her to know.

CHARLIE. I know.

GWEN. But someday, someday she's going to catch you.

CHARLIE. Yes, I suppose so.

GWEN. Why don't you just tell her that you have lady friends here and there?

CHARLIE. Because it's none of her business. Besides, she's too young to understand.

GWEN. Yes, my son too. Do you know where he thinks I am this afternoon? At the Garden Club learning how to get rid of aphids. Poor boy, he'd have apoplexy if he knew what I did for R and R. Why is it younger people and bureaucrats think desire ends at some arbitrary age?

CHARLIE. With bureaucrats it probably does.

(She smiles.)

And the young. How are they to know we don't feel on the inside like we look on the outside?

(Their eyes meet.)

GWEN. Well, it's been a lovely afternoon. But before I go, let me say it once again…

CHARLIE. You don't have to.

GWEN. I want to. After Walter ran off with that…that…

CHARLIE. Get it out.

GWEN. That…

(biting it out) younger woman!

CHARLIE. Again.

GWEN. *Younger* woman!

CHARLIE. Once more.

GWEN. No, I'm fine now… I was devastated. You helped me. I'll always be grateful for your friendship, your good humor and support, and for all the exciting conversation.

CHARLIE. Well, by the time you get to be sixty-seven you've learned to fake your way through a lot of subjects.

GWEN. And above all, Charlie, for moving mountains.

(He knows what she means, smiles.)

Now I better hurry home and pick up my macrame before my son gets in.

CHARLIE. Wait! The petitions!

(gets petitions for her)

Protect California forests… Ban drift-nets worldwide.

GWEN. I'll go to work on them right away. 'Bye, Charlie.
(light kiss) Thanks for the matinee.

*(**GWEN** goes. **CHARLIE** feels good. He goes to his computer, puts in some data.)*

*(**POLLY ADAMSON** appears in the courtyard. She would be coming from her condo which we do not see. She is 62, attractive, but dowdily dressed. **POLLY** is not actually timid, but she certainly is not assertive. Right now she is depressed.)*

(It shows all over her as she schleps along. To Charlie's

condo. Looks in. Knocks on the glass door to attract his attention. But by now **CHARLIE** *has finished with his computer, exits to the bathroom with his running clothes and shoes. Offstage he turns on the shower.)*

(For a moment **POLLY** *doesn't know what to do. She has to use the phone. So she comes in. She doesn't want to do so without permission, but by now – as she looks at the bathroom door –* **CHARLIE** *has begun to sing his version of "The Toreador Song" from Carmen. "Toreadora, don't spit on the floora. Use the cuspidora. That's what it's fora…" She makes up her mind. Goes to the phone, dials.)*

POLLY. Marc, please…Oh. May I leave a message for him?…Please tell him his Aunt Polly called. I've already moved. He'll understand. My phone is not in yet, but I would like to see him when it's convenient… Thank you.

(She hangs up, sighs heavily in her distress. Now a new burst of singing from **CHARLIE**, *as he finishes and turns off the shower. She opens her purse, takes out a coin and puts it by the phone. As she schlepped in, she schleps out.)*

(Now insistent buzzing of Charlie's door buzzer and pounding on the door. **CHARLIE** *comes in from bathroom, his running suit and shoes on, drying his hair, having heard the racket)*

CHARLIE. All right, all right, I'm coming!

(He crosses to door, opens it. It's **ELAINE***)*

I thought you had a million things to do.

ELAINE. *(comes in, all business)* Poppa, we have to talk. Who is she?

CHARLIE. Who?

ELAINE. The woman I saw coming out of your apartment.

CHARLIE. What woman?

ELAINE. The redhead, Poppa. She came sashaying out, all but skipping up the walk. If you have a lady friend, I think that's very nice. I'd like to meet her.

CHARLIE. You are mistaken.

ELAINE. I am not mistaken. I saw her.

CHARLIE. Are you going to believe me, your father, or what you see with your own eyes?

ELAINE. Poppa…!

CHARLIE. *(takes the offensive)* I am very disappointed in you. Yes, disappointed and ashamed. Spying on me.

ELAINE. I was not spying! I happened to be outside, talking to Mrs. Reed, the manager…

CHARLIE. I can't discuss this now. I have dishes to clean.

(He goes to the kitchen area to work on the dishes.)

ELAINE. You shouldn't let the dishes stack up like that.

CHARLIE. If you're going to start with the "shouldn'ts" *I'm* going out the door!

ELAINE. *(discovers empty champagne bottle)* Champagne.

CHARLIE. You caught me! I had a champagne brunch! Make me stand in the corner!

ELAINE. On Wednesday?! People don't have champagne brunches on Wednesdays. They have them on Sundays!

CHARLIE. I am not people! I am a senior citizen, retired! What ordinary people can only do on Sundays, I can do on Wednesdays! Or Fridays! Or Mondays! I am a totally free person! The conventions have nothing to do with me!

ELAINE. Poppa, I don't mean to pry…

CHARLIE. Like hell you don't!

ELAINE. Poppa, I have some powers of observation and the ability to deduce. The blinds were drawn, the bed was mussed, you were in your robe…

CHARLIE. I fail to see that as a federal offense.

ELAINE. Mrs. Reed said sometimes redheads come out, sometimes blondes, sometimes brunettes. I know you have many activities but I do not believe any of them is hairdressing.

CHARLIE. Elaine, please go home. Tell Bobby what to do. Tell Karen what to do. Tell George what to do…

ELAINE. I'm not trying to tell you what to do. I'm just trying to find out what you are doing! Who are they?

CHARLIE. Friends of mine.

ELAINE. Friends?

CHARLIE. Women I have met at the Center, in classes, on the beach.

ELAINE. The blondes, the brunettes, the redheads?

CHARLIE. Also grays with tinges of blue, orange with streaks of gold. Perhaps even a wig or two. I don't ask.

ELAINE. Then most of your friends are older women?

CHARLIE. Most of my friends are *mature* women, yes. And why is that?

    (his rage against nature)

Because there are many more mature women around than mature men. Look at the male! At the slightest provocation he rolls over on his back and sticks his legs up in the air! He withers right in front of your eyes and goes to powder! Is it my fault that nature is so discriminatory?

ELAINE. Poppa, I'm trying to understand all this.

CHARLIE. Don't bother. It'll be a terrible strain.

ELAINE. Mrs. Reed says you have a sin-bin here! That half the widows and divorcees in Santa Monica come visit!

CHARLIE. That is an exaggeration.

ELAINE. What isn't an exaggeration?

CHARLIE. I can't go into it now. I have envelopes to address.

    (He will go to his addressograph machine and begin to address envelopes.)

ELAINE. She says you are the Lothario of Ocean Boulevard. That you are the Don Juan, the Casanova, the Valentine of the neighborhood… She says you are a dirty old man!

CHARLIE. *(with restraint)* Mrs. Reed is a very nice person in her own way, but she has been known to sit under sea gulls without a hat.

ELAINE. Poppa…

CHARLIE. Oh, Elaine, for heaven sakes, wake up! Look around! See what I see!… Women strolling under parasols, walking dogs, riding bicycles… Marvelous, mature women. They have had experience. They have suffered and arrived at *a* depth of sensitivity not yet attained by their younger sisters. They are rivers that run deep. They know life before Rock and Roll. They have philosophy. They are of such varied backgrounds so as to make the variety endless. They are natural resources.

*(***POLLY*** *appears, schlepping her way from her place to the front of the complex. She plans to put her name on the mailbox. Exits.)*

They are a neglected garden in full bloom. They are single, they are lonely. And they don't care if my hair is styled or I wear Italian suits; they accept my natural self.

ELAINE. My God, Poppa, you have gone into the service business.

CHARLIE. I was lonely too! Miserably so! Your mother was not here! What is worse than loneliness? You need human skin to touch, breath to sense, someone to talk to in the middle of the night. You yourself is not enough. One is not a good number. It is close to zero. But two…three…four…

ELAINE. I'm mortified! My Poppa, a stud! You are almost seventy years old, you should have clicked off by now! I'm ashamed for people to know!

CHARLIE. Why? Because I have not seen enough, because I have not done enough! Elaine, this is the beach, one of God's supreme creations. That vast body of water, pulsating with life, crashes up against the rocks…

ELAINE. There are homeless on the grass…

CHARLIE. The sun up in the blue radiates warmth, palm trees sway in the breeze, flowers glorify the walks, fragrances everywhere…

ELAINE. And muggings in the street.

CHARLIE. Reality! It can ruin everybody's fun!

ELAINE. Poppa, please, don't get excited.

CHARLIE. I am excited! I'm pulsating too!… You know your trouble? You're an ageist!
(shows skin on his arm) Look! Wrinkles!
(shows skin on her arm) Smooth! Where is it written that smooth is better than wrinkles?!
(about her arm) Smooth is flat, smooth is boring! Wrinkles have texture, wrinkles have diversity! Why is the grape better than the raisin?
(shows back of her hand) Look! What do you see?

ELAINE. *(puzzled)* What? Nothing.

CHARLIE. Exactly!
(shows the back of his hand) Look! Liver spots! For added color! Elaine, the hair gets gray, the muscles don't do what they used to, flexibility goes, bones begin to scrape up against each other. But one thing, one thing remains.

ELAINE. I'm afraid to ask. What?

CHARLIE. Feeling. My friends and I are engaged in creative endeavor. I create feeling for someone; someone creates feeling for me. It is sort of like serving up nutrients. How can that be so bad?

ELAINE. I don't know, but it sounds like it should be.

CHARLIE. Why?! If I were forty years old, would I be a dirty middle-aged man? If I were twenty years old, would I be a dirty young man? All right. Same species, older edition.

ELAINE. That's it then! Senility! Senility has set in! Poppa, go see George. He'll know what to do.

CHARLIE. Oh, I know what he'll do! He'll operate!

ELAINE. Poppa, this needs expert opinion.

(CHARLIE is really wound up now.)

CHARLIE. Beware the expert! If the expert is so expert, why is it a new expert always comes along to correct the old expert?

ELAINE. But, Poppa, think...

CHARLIE. Don't think!! The cerebrum is *a* mixed blessing. It built the Taj Mahal and invented the sausage, but it also got people to think they were better than everybody else. I don't believe fish take on such airs.

ELAINE. No, they just eat each other.

CHARLIE. *(deep feeling about this)* Elaine, we are in an existence we haven't the vaguest idea what it is. So why do so many people try to tell everybody else how to live?

ELAINE. *(frustration)* Poppa, I don't know! I've got all I can do to take my pills in correct order!

(The door buzzer sounds. ELAINE peeks through blinds.)

It's the kid from up the block.

(She opens the door. The Kid says something we don't hear. Then:)

No, Charlie cannot come out and play.

(She shuts the door, sighs.) Poppa, half the time I don't know what you're talking about.

CHARLIE. *(tone changes)* I know. Daughter, I love you. I appreciate your concern for me, I really do. But...

(CHARLIE's fax machine starts.)

Excuse me. A message is coming in.

(crosses to fax machine)

ELAINE. Poppa, how many girlfriends do you have?

CHARLIE. I don't know. I don't count.

ELAINE. Estimate.

CHARLIE. More than one, less than five hundred.

ELAINE. Five hundred!

CHARLIE. There, you see, you have no sense of play! Go! Have your high tea...

ELAINE. Whatever the number, how do you keep track of them?

CHARLIE. I have a computer.

ELAINE. What?

CHARLIE. My memory may not be so good anymore. My computer remembers everything. I put data in. All on this disc.

(holds it up)

Vital statistics. Likes and dislikes. Does she like roses? Does she like broiled salmon? Does she like surprises? Should I prepare a feather? Names and occupations of children. Names and ages of grandchildren. Does she like a little S, does she like a little M?

ELAINE. Poppa, if you're trying to shock me, it's working.

CHARLIE. Will she sing gypsy songs? Will she sing Protestant hymns?

ELAINE. Hymns??

CHARLIE. Sometimes, I am told, the experience is heavenly.

ELAINE. I see.

CHARLIE. You see, you see! You don't see anything! All you can think about is sex.

(takes fax message)

The Center's monthly schedule. Excuse me, I have to make a call.

(will begin to ring a number)

ELAINE. What should I be thinking about?

CHARLIE. The friendship, the companionship, the mutual assistance, the conversation. She says what hurts her, I say what hurts me. She says what hurts her. I say what hurts me… Each is allowed three hurts, then conversation must change.

ELAINE. To what?

CHARLIE. To what doesn't hurt. That's the short part of the talk.

ELAINE. Poppa, you are toying with me. You are not serious.

CHARLIE. How can I be? You're so narrow.

ELAINE. I'm worried about you, that's all! I don't want anybody to get into trouble.

CHARLIE. Don't worry. Seniors get discounts on the pill.

ELAINE. I didn't mean that! I don't want you shot to death in a crime of passion!

CHARLIE. Way to go!

(into phone)

John…Charlie. The schedule's out. Alzheimer's Support Group, Friday, one o'clock… One o'clock…one o'clock. Right. How's Albert?… Good.

(hangs up)

John doesn't hear well. His wife has Alzheimer's. I drive them to the Center for the meetings.

(The information about John has a sobering effect on **ELAINE.***)*

Albert's a different case. His legs don't work right; he has trouble walking; his arms don't work right; he has trouble lifting. All he can do is make love. He does it lying down.

ELAINE. Poppa, I should think the women would want to get married. To have someone of their own.

CHARLIE. They don't. In most cases they wouldn't get a husband, they'd get a medical case.

ELAINE. And love? Doesn't love enter into it?

CHARLIE. Love. Yes, it is wonderful.- But it's for a different time, daughter. At this point, other things are far more important.

ELAINE. Like what?

CHARLIE. For one, compound interest. Now go meet Marsha.

ELAINE. I'll help you with the trash.

(She will take bundle of trash, exit rear of house.)

(In the courtyard **ROBERT ADAMSON** *appears. He is Polly's son, 39, carries an attache case. Robert wears glasses; his face is a bit off-center. He is a financial planner. Actually, as we shall learn, an amorous financial planner. He looks over at Charlie's place.)*

*(***CHARLIE***, meanwhile, has found the quarter* **POLLY** *left by his phone. Is puzzled by it. Pockets it as* **ROBERT** *knocks on glass door.)*

ROBERT. Hello.

CHARLIE. Hello.

ROBERT. My mother's moving into the complex. I wonder if you've seen her.

(is straining to see past **CHARLIE.** *into the condo)*

CHARLIE. No, I'm sorry.

ROBERT. *(about Charlie's place)* She's not in there, is she?

CHARLIE. Why would she be here…?

*(***ELAINE** *returns, sees* **ROBERT**, *is surprised)*

ELAINE. Robert!

ROBERT. Elaine!

(He crosses to her, looks into her face adoringly as he talks.)

ELAINE. What are you doing here?

ROBERT. I hoped I'd find you.

(aware **CHARLIE** *is looking)*

I mean…hello.

ELAINE. *(crosses from* **ROBERT***)* Poppa, this is Robert Adamson. He's George's and my financial planner…Charlie Fuller.

ROBERT. Hi.

CHARLIE. Hi.

(goes back to work on his addressograph machine)

ELAINE. *(hushed, to* **ROBERT***)* What are you doing here?

ROBERT. *(indicating off)* I bought the empty condo in back.

ELAINE. What?

ROBERT. For my mother. She's been rattling around the big old house ever since Dad died. I took an inventory of her life. She's not getting full use of her assets.

(CHARLIE *looks over at this.*)

George said your father loves it here, that it's a great complex, lots of activities for seniors... Mr. Fuller, can I take you into my confidence? Mom's really low. Dad died, she went into a shell. Stopped seeing her friends, stopped doing things. Maybe you could show her around, introduce her to people, get her into some activities...

ELAINE. *(is steps ahead; wanting to caution* ROBERT*)* Robert...

ROBERT. Your dad can be a great assist here.

(to CHARLIE*)*

That is, if you don't mind.

CHARLIE. *(the prospect of a new adventure)* Oh, no.

ELAINE. *(more urgently)* Robert...

CHARLIE. Your mother's welcome to join in on anything. Room for everybody. Here's the Center's schedule. "Shake, Rattle and Roll." That's earthquake preparedness. "Ethnic Cooking Classes." Political action: "How To Bang Heads With Your Congress Person"...

(A phone rings. Neither CHARLIE *nor* ELAINE *know from where. But* ROBERT *does. He says "Excuse me," opens his attache case and takes out the phone.)*

ROBERT. *(into phone)* Yes...Good. Fax to San Francisco. On the Ridley account?... What are you waiting for? Execute! Execute!
(hangs up) Sorry.

*(*ROBERT *will close his attache case. Meanwhile,* POLLY *comes back into the courtyard from her place. As before, heavy of heart, she schleps to Charlie's place. Knocks on glass.)*

POLLY. Hello.

(**CHARLIE** *turns, goes to her.*)

I'm sorry to bother you. I wonder if I could use your phone.

ROBERT. Mom!

POLLY. Robert! I was just going to call you.

ROBERT. Come in, come in! You won't believe the coincidence! This is Elaine Cooper. She and her husband, George, are clients of mine. This is her father. He lives here.

CHARLIE. Charlie. How do you do?

(*Slight pause as* **POLLY** *makes no reply.*)

ROBERT. Mom, tell him your name.

POLLY. What?

ROBERT. Your name, your name.

POLLY. Oh. I'm sorry, I'm so upset… Polly.

CHARLIE. Good! We're having a party! I'll put up some tea…

POLLY. (*outburst*) Robert, this isn't going to work!

ROBERT. It will, Mom, it will!

POLLY. I'm homesick.

ELAINE. Oh, the poor dear.

ROBERT. (*to* **ELAINE**) The drive from the big house to here is twenty-five minutes. She got homesick at the ten-minute mark… Mom, you'll get used to it, believe me.

POLLY. The walls are too close.

ROBERT. Why do you need big rooms? You're not going to play basketball! Mom, give it a chance.

ELAINE. Robert, how long has it been since your dad died?

POLLY. April.

ROBERT. Yes. Three years ago. She's usually not like this. She's usually more normal.

ELAINE. Well, she's frightened, that's understandable…

ROBERT. Why should she be? It's a security building. The neighborhood's good…

POLLY. But it's not the house!

ROBERT. No, Mom, but that's the beauty of it!
You move in here, the house goes up for sale, you get a one-time shelter of $250,000, put the proceeds into Treasuries, pay the rent to me as owner of the condo, I get a write-off...

*(**POLLY** lets out a wail, startling everybody.)*

POLLY. The place is no good!

ROBERT. What's the matter with it?

POLLY. I can't tell you.

ROBERT. Why not?

POLLY. Not in front of strangers.

ROBERT. They're not strangers, Mom, they're almost family...

POLLY. The toilet doesn't flush.

ROBERT. What?

POLLY. *(wailing)* It doesn't flush! I press the lever, nothing happens. I press the lever, nothing happens...

CHARLIE. That's nothing, Polly. The water's turned off. I can get it going in a minute.

ROBERT. Charlie says you're very welcome here. There are all kinds of activities...

CHARLIE. Sure! Polly, it's a terrific time in your life. You can do whatever you want. No boss to please, no spouse to consider, no kids to worry about. You. That's all there is, you.

*(to **ROBERT** and **ELAINE**)*

Oh, she'd be terrific undercover.

*(They look at **CHARLIE** startled. He explains.)*

Undercover. A secret agent. You see, there are a lot of crumbbums around cheating seniors. They get unsuspecting, trusting people, mostly widows, and screw them over. They misrepresent things they sell. They twist a person out of a good insurance policy into a bad one. I work with AARP. That's the American Association of

Retired People. We use undercover agents, wire them, tape the sales pitch those creeps make and then turn them over to the Bunco Squad!

ROBERT. Hey, that sounds exciting!

POLLY. Oh, I could never do that.

CHARLIE. Sure you could. I'll show you how.

(gets wrench) Come on, I'll turn on your water.

*(**POLLY** hesitates. Looks at **ROBERT**.)*

ROBERT. Go on, Mom.

*(**POLLY** starts out. **CHARLIE** hangs back a moment.)*

CHARLIE. *(sotto; to **ROBERT** and **ELAINE**)* She's perfect for undercover. She's as helpless as they come.

*(**CHARLIE** joins **POLLY** near glass door.)*

POLLY. Did you get my quarter?

CHARLIE. What?

POLLY. I phoned my nephew, Marc, and left you a quarter.

CHARLIE. Oh, that was your quarter. Here, take it back. My treat.

*(They exit. **ROBERT** immediately moves close to **ELAINE**. Into her face:)*

ROBERT. I confess. I want Mom here so I have an excuse to come over and see you.

*(Though **ELAINE** protests vehemently to **ROBERT**'s advances, secretly she enjoys them.)*

ELAINE. Oh, you're so rotten!

(crosses from him)

ROBERT. *(crosses after her)* You visit your father, I visit my mother. See the synergy here?

ELAINE. Rotten, rotten, rotten!

(crosses from him)

Robert, you're going to have to stop this!

ROBERT. *(a desperate man)* How can I?! I dream about you every night! Torrid dreams! Wicked dreams! Delicious dreams! I have to keep a distance from my wife or she will expect a midnight surprise.

ELAINE. That's her right! It's mean of you to deprive her!

ROBERT. I know, but I'm helpless...

ELAINE. Don't touch me!

(crossing from him)

This is ridiculous! You have a wife, I have a husband! You have children, I have children...

ROBERT. You have a father, I have a mother! Just because we have relatives, does that mean life ends? You have a cat, I have a dog! I don't see that as significant!... Look at your life. Check your free cash flow. Can you say you're operating in the black... Look at me! Annual reports! P&Ls, R&Ds, M&As! CMOs, LBOs! 10-Ks and 10-Qs! Thirty-nine years old, my life is almost over!... This little deal between us can be the sweetener! It's a win-win situation!

ELAINE. Touch me again, I'll tell George!

ROBERT. You can't! You won't! Elaine, please listen. From the first moment I saw you I've been crazy about your bottom line!

ELAINE. *(crossing from him)* I can't talk about this a moment longer! I'm redoing my kitchen!

ROBERT. I'll help!

ELAINE. I have to decide on the counter-tops. European tile or granite?

ROBERT. I'll do a feasibility study!

ELAINE. On the surface units. Gas or electricity?

ROBERT. I'll do an environmental impact! See the cross-collateralization here!

ELAINE. Oh, you're so bad!

ROBERT. I know. I have my shortcomings.

ELAINE. If you weren't so good at making money for us I'd have George rescind our discretionary account immediately!

(CHARLIE and POLLY appear in the courtyard. He is looking at Polly's album of family pictures. They enter.)

CHARLIE. *(astonished at what he sees)* That's you!

POLLY. Yes.

CHARLIE. At 16! All the boys must have been falling all over themselves to get near you.

POLLY. *(flattered)* Well...

CHARLIE. Look! You were Prom Queen!

POLLY. Well, a Princess.

CHARLIE. You should have been Queen.

POLLY. *(laughing, pleased)* Oh, Charlie.

ROBERT. *(surprised)* Mom, you're laughing!

POLLY. I am? *(realizing she was)* I am.

CHARLIE. Oh, sure, we've become good friends already. *(kisses her hand)*

POLLY. *(embarrassed, but thrilled)* Charlie!

CHARLIE. *(with no implication)* Don't worry about a thing, Robert! We'll do all we can to see that your mother gets full use of her assets!

(gets string bag; to POLLY) String bag! Come on!

ELAINE. Where are you going?

CHARLIE. To the market to pick up some things for Polly's refrigerator.

(Has fetched a helmet which he gives to her.)

Here, put this on.

POLLY. *(holds helmet)* What for?

CHARLIE. You can't ride my moped without one.

POLLY. But I'm not riding a moped.

CHARLIE. Of course you are. It's easy. *(gets his helmet)*

POLLY. But...I never rode one before.

CHARLIE. Good! A new experience. It'll bring out the gypsy in you. Time to do things you've never done before, but thought about! Time to fulfill dreams! If not now, when! If not now, never!

(He puts on his helmet.)

POLLY. Oh, I never did that before.

CHARLIE. Well, you're doing it now!

(He has taken her helmet and puts it on her head... leads her out. In a moment, as **ELAINE** *and* **ROBERT** *look out, we hear:)*

CHARLIE. Hop on!

POLLY. Oh, I never did this before!

(now the whoosh of the moped)

POLLY. Oh, I never did this before!

(and they're gone)

(blackout)

Scene Two

(The same. Some days later. **CHARLIE** *is alone, fiddling with dark-framed glasses, as he waits for* **POLLY**...*who enters. Her clothing has made a pronounced change – from dowdy to beach attire. And she shows much more vitality.)*

CHARLIE. All right, let's practice.

(This is pretending.)

You have the wire under your shirt. Here, put this sweater on. It covers better.

POLLY. *(puts on sweater)* Oh, this is so exciting! Do you think I can do it?

CHARLIE. Sure! Look at how changed you are in so short a time.

POLLY Oh, I never did this before!

CHARLIE. You're a widow. Elderly. Vulnerable.

POLLY. Dumb.

CHARLIE. You don't have to be dumb. Elderly and vulnerable are enough. I'm the dirty sonofabitch who's trying to screw you.

POLLY. I know!... I've been warned. Elaine says you're a fox. Mrs. Reed says you're a wolf...

*(***CHARLIE*** fixes her with a look.)*

Sorry. You're the insurance salesman who's trying to rip me off.

(The eyeglasses are the prop that makes **CHARLIE** *"the insurance man.")*

CHARLIE. Conservative, dress. Neat haircut. The All-American look. Honest. Sincere. I could be a member of your church. In fact, in many instances, I am.

POLLY. *(looks at her wristwatch)* I wonder where Marc is. He said he'd be here by now.

CHARLIE. Maybe his plane's late.

POLLY. He's very anxious to meet you. I've told him so much about you…

CHARLIE. Polly, are we doing this or not?

POLLY. Ready!

(He exits. Door is shut. He knocks on it. She opens it. He wears the dark-rimmed eyeglasses.)

CHARLIE. *(playing the part)* Thank you, Mrs. Adamson, for agreeing to meet me.

POLLY. *(playing the part)* Well, after all, it may be for my benefit.

CHARLIE. Perfect! Just the right tone. Remember, don't say too much, you're shy.

POLLY. Oh, this is so exciting!

CHARLIE. The sonofabitch'll ask you about your grandchildren. He'll want to see pictures. You'll show them. He'll "ooh" and "aah."

POLLY. *(playing the part)* Thank you. They're such good youngsters.

CHARLIE. Fantastic! All right, now that he's buttered you, he puts you on the frying pan.
(playing the part) Oh, yes, I happen to be familiar with that policy you have. Not bad, not bad at all. A little out of date, of course. You see, we have new products that target the problem of long-term health care head-on…
(out of the part) Blab, blab, blab, he'll go into a lot of gobbledygook you won't understand, but that's what we want on the tape, the pitch!

POLLY. *(playing the part)* Oh, I'm so grateful for you taking this time with me.

CHARLIE. Incredible! Polly, you're a natural!

POLLY. How do you know so much about insurance men?

CHARLIE. I used to be one. I had my own agency in L.A. Now he starts twisting you.

POLLY. I'm ready for him!

CHARLIE. *(playing the part)* So actually there's no comparison between what you now have and what you can have at no extra cost.

POLLY. *(playing the part)* Yes, I can see that.

CHARLIE. *(playing the part)* Oh, you're very sharp, Mrs. Adamson. You caught on right away. So you just let your policy lapse, save on the premium, sign up for this one. That's all there is to it.

POLLY. *(playing the part)* Well, I really think I ought to talk to someone about it.

CHARLIE. Fabulous! Great touch! Suck him in deeper.

(playing the part) Oh, certainly, certainly.

The thing is, however, if you write the check now you can take advantage of the one-time special price and, you won't believe this, the medical examination is waived!

POLLY. Really?

CHARLIE. *(pantomimes)* Here. Use my pen.

POLLY. *(sudden outburst)* OH, YOU SONOFABITCH! HOW DARE YOU TRY TO RIP ME OFF LIKE THAT...!

*(**CHARLIE** is startled.)*

YOU THINK I'M STUPID BECAUSE I'M AN ELDERLY, VULNERABLE WIDOW...!

CHARLIE. *(overriding)* No, no, no! You can't do that! You don't want him to know you know!

POLLY. Oh, I'm sorry, Charlie. It seemed so real.

CHARLIE. Polly, you can't lose concentration or you'll blow it.

POLLY. I know. Oh, I don't think I can do this...

CHARLIE. Yes, yes, you can! You can do anything! You can move mountains!

*(**CHARLIE** finds himself looking into her face. **POLLY** notices it. He turns away.)*

Let's take a break.

(The phone rings.)

Excuse me.

(answers phone)

CHARLIE. *(cont.)* Hello… Oh, it's you… Yes, Elaine, she *is* here… It's no business of yours what we're doing!… All right, all right, we're playing doctor! Now are you satisfied?… Hold on, a call's coming in.

(clicks on new call) Hello… Oh, it's you… Hold on.

(clicks back to **ELAINE***)*

It's Robert. He wants to know if you're here… Hold on.

(clicks back to **ROBERT***)*

She wants me to tell you she's not here which I was going to do since she isn't… Hold on.

(clicks back to **ELAINE***)*

He wants to know when you'll be here.

(Listens. Clicks back to **ROBERT***.)*

She doesn't know and even if she did she wouldn't tell you.

(sudden realization) What am I doing?!

(He bangs down phone. Instantly it rings. He pulls phone jack out of the wall.)

Let's do pasta!

POLLY. Good! I've been studying!

(They cross to computer. **CHARLIE** *will activate it.)*

CHARLIE. All right, I'll call up the graphics. You identify them. But no ravioli or macaroni. They're too easy.

(calls up a graphic) Slightly curved tubes. Ridges.

POLLY. Rigatoni.

CHARLIE. *(works button, another graphic)* Not curved. Larger.

POLLY. Ditali.

CHARLIE. *(another graphic)* Spaghetti that's hollow.

POLLY. Bucatini.

CHARLIE. *(another graphic)* Bow tie.

POLLY. Farfalle!

CHARLIE. Correct, correct, correct! Before you know it you'll be an Italian chef yourself!

POLLY. Oh, Charlie, I'm enjoying it here! I didn't think I would. But the people I've met, the things there are to do.

CHARLIE. It's been wonderful having you here. There's something…different about you.

POLLY. Thank you. I must have been some kind of drip when I first moved in.

CHARLIE. You were frightened, that's all. It's natural. You lived one way for a long time, it's hard to make changes.

POLLY. *(Charlie's influence already)* But we have to!

CHARLIE. You're doing it! *I* think Ralph would be very pleased. He'd be happy knowing you're doing so well! *(works buttons, another graphic)* All right, here come the toughies. Snail shape.

POLLY. Lumache!

CHARLIE. *(another graphic)* Tiny rings!

POLLY. Anelli!

CHARLIE. *(another graphic)* Smooth. Short.

POLLY. Ziti!

CHARLIE. *(another graphic)* Wide. Wavy.

POLLY. Tagliatelli!

    *(as **CHARLIE** works buttons)* Conchiglie!

    *(as **CHARLIE** works buttons)* Nancy Ryan. Don't forget the feather.

    *(**POLLY** looks at **CHARLIE**, puzzled.)*

CHARLIE. Sorry. Mixup.

    (works the buttons) Here, try this one.

POLLY. Charlie, it's really true, isn't it?

CHARLIE. What?

POLLY. What Elaine says about you, what Mrs. Reed says about you. Oh, I'm not passing moral judgment. It's just interesting, that's all. Have you always been…that way?

CHARLIE. *(adamant)* No, no! Not while Grace was alive, never!

POLLY. Oh, I see. Then maybe it's some kind of post-mortem depression.

CHARLIE. *(back to the pasta test, quickly)* Spiral shape!

POLLY. Fusilli!

CHARLIE. One hundred percent! You have just won the Garibaldi Medal for Pasta Identification! I'm required to kiss you on both cheeks!

(He does so. A moment of warmth between them.)

POLLY. *(not critically)* Charlie, my cheeks don't go that low. You kissed my neck.

CHARLIE. I have to tell you the truth. It was on purpose.

POLLY. Oh, you're such a sly old goat.

CHARLIE. A fox, a wolf, a goat! All by myself I'm the whole San Diego Zoo!

POLLY. Charlie, I like you as a friend very much. I like your spirit and so many of the things you say about dreams, about fulfilling fantasies, but I'm not going to become part of your harem.

CHARLIE. Thank God! For a moment there I thought you were weakening!

POLLY. Oh, you're not going to fool me with your tricks.

CHARLIE. Polly, you can be a most exasperating woman!

POLLY. Yes, Ralph used to say that too. Maybe it's true.

(stops; softly, ruefully) Charlie, I miss him.

CHARLIE. *(softly, ruefully)* I know. I miss her too.

POLLY. He was a wonderful person.

CHARLIE. Grace too.

POLLY. There were so many nice things about him. He was a good provider, he was a wonderful father.

CHARLIE. Grace too. A mother.

POLLY. In fact, he was so wonderful I'd often forget what a stinker he could be too...Oh, it was so irritating! It was so humiliating! He'd explain the simplest of things to

me over and over as though I didn't know anything!
He'd correct me in public! There we'd be with a group
of people. I'd tell a story. He'd correct me right there
and then! I hated that! So what if I were a little wrong?
He shouldn't embarrass me! If you make a fool of
yourself that's all right; if someone else makes a fool of
you that's not very nice! Oh what is it with...*you men?*
You have to be such know-it-alls! I couldn't fight back.
(demonstrates) I used to give him the finger behind my
hand.

CHARLIE. *(sympathetic)* Yes. Grace had her faults too. She
left me.

POLLY. I didn't know that. I thought she died.

CHARLIE. Oh, yes, but that was later. Dumped me. Just
dumped me. I never could figure out why. Then it
happened. Suddenly. Before we had a chance to get
back together. A car jumped the curb...

POLLY. Oh, Charlie, that's terrible! I'm so sorry.

(**CHARLIE** *nods.*)

With Ralph it was very slow. Very, very slow and very,
very painful.

CHARLIE. *(sudden outburst)* Damn! That's one of my quar-
rels with God! Damn, damn, damn!

POLLY. *(stunned by his outburst)* Charlie...

CHARLIE. Why does it have to be so tough?! I'll tell you
why! Because it wasn't God! God would not have left
out fairness! When He decided to create the earth I
think He picked the wrong subcontractor...I don't
like to say He's cheap, but I think He went for the
lowest bidder.

POLLY. Charlie, that's a very strange thing to say.

CHARLIE. Come to think of it, what's sillier than the universe
anyway? A bunch of rocks floating around in empty
space waiting to congeal. Who can take it seriously?

POLLY. Charlie, there's a design to things and meaning.
Oh, Ralph would certainly have given you an argu-
ment on that.

CHARLIE. Grace did. She was very religious.

POLLY. Ralph too. Not that he went to church or practiced it very much, but he did believe in the Ten Commandments.

CHARLIE. Me too! But nine out of ten is still a pretty good score.

POLLY. That, I believe, Ralph would have agreed with.

(no anger here)

You see, he screwed around a lot.

CHARLIE. No!

POLLY. He traveled on business. For G.E. and developed an interest in airline stewardesses. Oh, I can talk about it now. It doesn't hurt anymore. Airline stewardesses! What's the big thing about them?

CHARLIE. Well, they fly in…but they also fly out.

POLLY. Oh, I see. I never thought of it that way.

CHARLIE. It's the same with women as men. Some women you meet are four-hour women and some are weekend women, some even are women of the month. But the rare ones are the open-ended women, no time limit.

(They are looking at each other, a bit more seriously than before.)

POLLY. Yes, I can understand that.

CHARLIE. Polly, I have to tell you something. I like women who look like you and frankly, you're the only one I've found that way.

POLLY. Oh, what a sweet thing to say.

*(**CHARLIE** smiles, thinks he has made points.)*

And it's so practical. You can use that line on any woman.

CHARLIE. Damn, damn! Ralph was right! You *are* an exasperating woman.

(The door buzzer sounds.)

POLLY. That's Marc!

(She crosses to door, opens it on **MARC**.…*34, tall, good-looking, in a TWA flight crew uniform. He carries a huge bouquet of flowers.)*

POLLY. *(cont.)* Marc!

MARC. Hi, Aunt Polly.

POLLY. *(about flowers)* So many!

MARC. Hi, I'm Marc.

CHARLIE. Charlie.

(They shake hands.)

MARC. Sorry I'm late. I tried to phone, but I couldn't get through.

(sees phone)

No wonder! The jack's out of the wall. Here, I'll put it back. in.

(He does so. Phone rings immediately. Answering machine picks up call.)

CHARLIE'S VOICE. Charlie Fuller. Please speak.

LILY'S VOICE. *(warmly)* Charlie, this is Lily. About Sunday…

*(**CHARLIE** pulls phone jack out of wall.)*

CHARLIE. It's better this way.

MARC. Aunt Polly, I can't stay.

(re: phone)

That's why I tried so hard to reach you. I've got to fill in on the London flight.

POLLY. Oh, Marc, I thought we'd have time to visit.

MARC. Me too. Next time, I promise… Great place you've got here, Mr. Fuller.

CHARLIE. Charlie… Thanks.

MARC. Aunt Polly's told me so much about you…

CHARLIE. You too. You're her favorite relative…

POLLY. You two get acquainted. I'll go put these in water.

MARC. I'll help you…

POLLY. No, no, I'll be right back. Charlie's brewed some tea. You've got time for a cup at least.

*(She goes. **CHARLIE** moves to the kitchen area, will pour tea. **MARC**, meanwhile, looks after **POLLY**. Makes sure she's gone, then suddenly turns serious.)*

MARC. I'm glad she left us alone. I don't want her to hear this.

*(**CHARLIE** looks at him.)*

Let's see. How do I begin?

CHARLIE. Jump in!

MARC. Good advice!

(but still can't get to it)

Well, let's see. Charlie, you're an older person. Life smart. You've seen things, learned about people. Actually, from what I hear, you're a genius!

CHARLIE. *(modestly)* Oh, no…

MARC. It's true!…

*(About **CHARLIE** pouring tea. Showing some of his desperation)*

…Charlie, I don't want to seem ungrateful, but I don't need tea. What *I* need is advice. I've met this woman. Wonderful woman! Lovely, warm, witty, genuine, comfortable to be with.

CHARLIE. That doesn't sound like a problem.

MARC. When I'm in town, she'll have lunch with me, go to a movie. She'll laugh at my jokes, straighten my tie, brush back my hair; but that's all! Every time I make a serious move, she hits the reject button.

CHARLIE. *That* is a problem.

MARC. *(a desperate man)* I do all the things the magazines say to do! Be assertive, I'm assertive! Be decisive, I'm decisive! Be gentle…if only I had the chance! I try to cover all the bases and what!

CHARLIE. What?

MARC. *(hits the reject button)* Reject!… So I implore!

CHARLIE. Don't implore!

MARC. I ignore!

CHARLIE. Don't ignore!

MARC. I mope, I bristle…!

CHARLIE. No, no! Don't do either!

MARC. Well, I can see I'm doing it all wrong. I feel awful, Charlie. I absolutely adore her.

(**CHARLIE** *is very compassionate toward* **MARC**. *Pats him.*)

CHARLIE. Yes, yes, I know. It's tricky stuff. If she can push you around too easily, you're a wimp. If she can't push you around at all, you're a brute.

MARC. That leaves very little margin for error.

CHARLIE. The woman is a fastidious person, Marc. She draws a very fine line.

MARC. Then what am I to do? I navigate the plane for Rome. I start thinking about her. If I'm not careful we end up in Helsinki.

CHARLIE. Older men, younger men. The problem is the same. This may surprise you, but I have met a woman too.

MARC. No!

CHARLIE. Just as you say. Lovely, warm, witty, genuine, comfortable to be with.

MARC. One of a kind!

CHARLIE. That's it!

MARC. You feel about her as you've never felt about another woman!

CHARLIE. Exactly!

MARC. It could be bliss, it could be nirvana! But you make a move one way, she blocks you. You make a move another way, she blocks you!

CHARLIE. Yes!

MARC. Exasperating!

CHARLIE. You could kill!

MARC. That's it, Charlie. We're in love.

CHARLIE. No!!

MARC. Yes, Charlie, that's how it works…What am I going to do, tell me!

CHARLIE. What can I tell you? Science has shown that men think of sex every minute, women every ten minutes. The question is, how do you handle the nine minutes in between?

MARC. How??

CHARLIE. All I can say to you is what I say to myself. Men don't like to hear this, but the woman is steps ahead. She knows how it will end even before he knows there's a road to travel. He can prance and flex and cock-a-doodle-doo all over the place. He can build the bridges and shoot the cannon, but she…she, in her quiet way, will set the course. If she wants, you will. If she doesn't, short of drugging her, you won't.

MARC. That's terrible! It makes it all so hopeless!
What good are all those "how to" books? Where is aggressiveness? What good is macho??

CHARLIE. Good, very good! But paying attention is better.

(pats **MARC***)*

So stay optimistic, my boy. Keep the corners of your mouth up! Attitude is everything!

MARC. Meanwhile, I'm in a holding pattern.

CHARLIE. Ever-ready should you get the call! You're a fine-looking, intelligent young man. I predict success. Soon I expect to see a smile on your lips and a bounce to your step.

*(***POLLY*** *is returning.* **CHARLIE** *sees her in courtyard, turns the subject as she comes in.)*

Well, I'm sorry you can't stay longer, Marc. Next time.

POLLY. My place smells like a florist shop! I love it!

MARC. Well, I hate to do it, but duty calls. It's been a real pleasure meeting you.

CHARLIE. I hope to see you again soon. He's a fine young man, Polly.

POLLY. I think so.

MARC. I'll try to make it back for your birthday, Aunt Polly. We'll celebrate.

POLLY. That would be wonderful.

(She kisses him on the cheek. He goes. A dreamy quality comes over **POLLY**. *Actually, something deep inside her is taking place. She is coming to some kind of conclusion. Meanwhile:)*

CHARLIE. Your birthday? When's that?

POLLY. Next Thursday.

CHARLIE. You didn't say anything. How old?…Lie.

POLLY. Fifty-nine…That's the lie.

CHARLIE. I knew it!…Older or younger?

POLLY. Oh, Charlie! Sixty-two. Exactly.

CHARLIE. A perfect age for an Italian dinner! I will make it! I've got a sauce *(kisses his fingers)* that takes fourteen hours to make! I won't take "no" now that it's an occasion!

POLLY. *(simply)* All right.

CHARLIE. *(Did he hear her correctly?)* All right?

POLLY. *(softly)* Yes.

(Their relationship has moved to a different plane.)

CHARLIE. I've got a birthday present for you already!

(He gives her a book. She looks at the dust cover.)

POLLY. "The Fine Art of Italian Cooking"?

CHARLIE. That's just the dust cover. As with people, it's not the same on the inside as the outside.

*(***POLLY** *opens the book again.)*

POLLY. "The Joy of Sex."

(She closes book.)

CHARLIE. A little light bedtime reading. Of course, if you'd rather have the book that comes with the dust cover…

(He reaches for the book. She pulls it away from him. He laughs: A-hah! She wants the book.)

POLLY. It is not gracious to refuse a birthday gift as given. I have to go now, Charlie.

CHARLIE. Then we're on for Thursday night.

POLLY. Oh, yes.

*(**POLLY** goes, holding the book. **CHARLIE** looks after her. He's ecstatic; he's got it made. He sails across the room, jumps up and clicks his heels.)*

(blackout)

Scene Three

(The same. Evening. Thursday. The room has been arranged for the dinner. The table is set with Charlie's best. Candles. Ice bucket. Flowers. A stream of letters strung along the wall reading HAPPY BIRTHDAY.)

*(Initially the stage is empty. We hear **CHARLIE** stirring in the back. After a moment he appears, singing a Italian song. He wears a cook's hat and a smock that covers all his clothing. He is doing his last minute fussing with pots and pans. He is feeling great. He checks his wristwatch. It's getting to be that time. He pulls off his cook's hat, tosses it aside. He pulls off his smock revealing his dress: black tie. Tuxedo, crisp white shirt, French cuff links. He fusses a bit with his clothes. Now he gets a champagne bottle [the Flower Bottle], puts it in the ice bucket, stirs it, puts a towel over it. He lights the candles.)*

*(The door buzzer sounds. That's it! It's **POLLY**!)*

CHARLIE. Coming!

*(He turns down the lights. It's all so romantic. He glides to the door, opens it. But it's not **POLLY**, it's **ELAINE**.)*

ELAINE. *(bursts in)* He's not here, is he?

CHARLIE. Who?

ELAINE. Robert, Robert! He pops up wherever I go! How does he do it! I think he's attached a homing device to me somehow! Poppa, it's so dark.

(She flicks on the lights. Sees him in a tuxedo, is surprised.)

Poppa! You look wonderful!

CHARLIE. Thank you.

ELAINE. *(suspicious)* Why are you wearing it?

CHARLIE. Oh, it's just a little nothing that was hanging in the closet.

ELAINE. *(sniffing)* Cooking? I smell cooking?

(seeing) Candles! Happy Birthday! Happy Birthday who?

CHARLIE. None of your business.

ELAINE. If I punch up your computer, will it tell me whose birthday it is?

CHARLIE. Elaine, please leave. I'm expecting a guest any minute.

ELAINE. *(about the whole scene)* So this is how you do it! The Venus Flytrap!

CHARLIE. This is no flytrap! This is a man and a woman having a little celebratory dinner. Now go…

(Suddenly **ELAINE** *breaks.)*

ELAINE. Oh, Poppa, I'm so miserable.

CHARLIE. *(genuinely concerned)* What?

ELAINE. Miserable, miserable, miserable. I don't know what to do.

CHARLIE. Elaine, what is it?

ELAINE. Oh, how do I begin?

CHARLIE. Jump in!

ELAINE. Yes, yes, that's a good way. Poppa, you're smart. Yes, you really are. I need advice.

CHARLIE. Elaine, what is it?

ELAINE. George. He's having an affair.

CHARLIE. No.

ELAINE. Yes.

CHARLIE. With whom?

ELAINE. His endodontist.

CHARLIE. *(That's hard to believe.)* George is having an affair with his endodontist? How can he get passionate over someone giving him a root canal? No, no, you're mistaken. That can't be.

ELAINE. It is! I saw them together in this very romantic French restaurant.

CHARLIE. What were you doing there?

ELAINE. Robert took me.

CHARLIE. What?

ELAINE. Oh, it was perfectly innocent. I had this yen for a cassoulet.

CHARLIE. Then maybe George had a yen for a cassoulet too!

ELAINE. No, I saw them holding hands under the table. Robert never so much as touched my hand! I wouldn't permit it! Naturally, I left the restaurant immediately before George could see me...

CHARLIE. *(has no time for this; looks at his watch)* Elaine, please, can we talk about this tomorrow...?

ELAINE. *(the little child)* Poppa...

CHARLIE. Daughter, I love you. I stopped worrying about you when you got married. But if you want me to, I'll start again.

ELAINE. Would you, Poppa?

CHARLIE. *(firmly)* Yes, yes, I will!...But not right now.

*(The door buzzer sounds. **CHARLIE** jumps.)*

It's she!! Elaine, you've got to get out of here.

*(**ELAINE**, meanwhile, has gone to the window, peeks out.)*

ELAINE. It's Robert! He followed me here! I can't see him! I have to hide!

(looks around)

CHARLIE. Don't hide!

ELAINE. The sauna!

CHARLIE. Not the sauna!

*(But **ELAINE** is already heading for the sauna and goes in. Meanwhile, door buzzer keeps up.)*

All right, all right, I'm coming!

*(He crosses to door. Opens it. **ROBERT** bursts in, carrying his attache case.)*

ROBERT. Elaine, Elaine, is she here? I was sure she came here.

CHARLIE. You can see for yourself.

ROBERT. I've got to talk to her! It can't go on this way! It's preposterous!

(suddenly aware) You look different.

CHARLIE. Do I?

ROBERT. Yes. There's something different about you.

CHARLIE. Guess.

ROBERT. You got a haircut!

CHARLIE. That's it! Robert, I can't talk to you now. I'm very busy.

ROBERT. *(breaks)* Oh, I'm so depressed. I'm drowning in red ink. I don't know what to do.

*(**CHARLIE***'s shoulders sag. Another one.)*

How can I tell you? How do I begin?…Okay, I'll jump in.

CHARLIE. Don't jump in!

ROBERT. Charlie, you're a master…

CHARLIE. I'm not a master!

ROBERT. I need your advice.

CHARLIE. I don't have any!

ROBERT. It's Elaine.

(indecisive) Should I tell you?

(decisive) Okay, I'll tell you. It's really about George. He's having an affair with his periodontist.

CHARLIE. No, it's his endodontist.

ROBERT. No, he went from endo to perio.

CHARLIE. Well, there's a man who likes women who know their way around a mouth. Robert, I can't help you. I've got the evening planned…

ROBERT. *(seeing the lettering)* Happy Birthday! It's my mother's birthday.

CHARLIE. Yes, yes, it is.

ROBERT. You're having dinner with her.

CHARLIE. Yes, I am.

ROBERT. *(realizing now)* It's not the haircut! It's your tuxedo!

CHARLIE. Bingo!

ROBERT. Champagne! Candlelight! I'll bet you've got an Italian love song on the stereo!

CHARLIE. Well…

(**ROBERT** *flicks on the stereo. Sure enough the room is filled with music: THE ITALIAN TENOR'S SONG in Richard Strauss' Der Rosenkavalier.*)

ROBERT. Charlie.

(wagging finger at him) Charlie, Charlie, Charlie.

CHARLIE. Now just a minute. Don't get the wrong idea.

ROBERT. Well, I haven't been able to have an affair. Maybe my mother can.

(door buzzer sounds)

CHARLIE. It's she!!

ROBERT. Oh, I don't want her to see me here! I've got to hide!

CHARLIE. Don't hide!

ROBERT. I know! The sauna!

CHARLIE. Not the sauna!

(*But* **ROBERT** *has already bolted into the sauna with his attache case. Meanwhile, the door buzzer keeps up.*)

All right, all right, I'm coming!

(*He crosses to door. Adjusts his clothes for* **POLLY**. *Opens door.* **HARRIET**, *69, sticks her head in. She wears a light topcoat.*)

HARRIET. *(sings)* "Rock of Ages, cleft for me."

CHARLIE. Harriet!

HARRIET. *(comes in, singing)* "Let me hide myself in thee." Third Thursday of the month, Harriet's night!

CHARLIE. *(to himself)* Oh, my God, I forgot.

HARRIET. Look, Charlie, I went to the Trashy Lingerie Shoppe.

(*She opens her topcoat to reveal herself in trashy lingerie. Black and red lace, garters, etc.*)

I can't wear this anyplace but here. How do I look?

CHARLIE. *(dryly)* The shop is correctly named.

HARRIET. Yes. Disgusting, isn't it? Well, every fantasy can't work out...Lily Carter was at the shop buying things. She's the only nympho I know who hasn't burnt out with age.

(There is a rumble in the sauna.) What's that?

CHARLIE. Nothing, nothing. Harriet...

HARRIET. *(sees the lettering)* Happy Birthday! You remembered it's my birthday!

(**CHARLIE** *looks puzzled. There's something wrong with that.*)

Oh, Charlie, that's'so dear of you!

CHARLIE. It's not your birthday.

(goes to computer, calls up data)

HARRIET. Well, not today exactly.

CHARLIE. Not today exactly.

(indicates monitor) February 10! Six months from now!

(Now an abrupt change in **HARRIET**. *Not anger, not accusation. Simple acceptance.)*

HARRIET. I thought it might have been an innocent mistake. But it's no mistake, is it, Charlie? So if it isn't my birthday and that says "Happy Birthday" then obviously *(indicates the romantic scene)* this isn't for me.

(**CHARLIE** *understands her feeling and is contrite)*

CHARLIE. I'm sorry, Harriet...

HARRIET. *(in pain)* How could you, Charlie? The third Thursday of the month. I looked forward to it. I dreamed about it. The night before I could hardly sleep...You never got mixed up before. It's the new girl on the block, isn't it?

CHARLIE. *(squirming)* Harriet...

HARRIET. Well, I expected it sooner or later. But not this way. Not a cold, wet towel in the face. Where's the grace? When you dumped me I always thought it would be with the Charlie Fuller finesse so there'd be no pain.

(In the sauna a phone rings. **HARRIET** *looks over, puzzled.)*

HARRIET. *(cont.)* Do you have a phone in the sauna?

CHARLIE. No, no…

(now a bigger rumble in the sauna)

HARRIET. What the hell is that?!

(Out of the sauna bursts **ELAINE**, *her clothing all but torn off. She is followed by* **ROBERT**, *carrying his attache case, the phone inside ringing.)*

ELAINE. Beast! Degenerate! Satyr!

ROBERT. *(pursuing her)* Darling! Sweetheart! Hear me!

ELAINE. If you don't stop pursuing me I'm going to get a gun and shoot you!

(exits)

ROBERT. At least the bullet would be yours!

(ROBERT *starts after her. Stops as he sees* **HARRIET** *who has closed her topcoat…Now as* **ROBERT** *looks at her, she opens her coat, revealing her trashy lingerie for* **ROBERT** *to see. He looks puzzled, then:)*

ROBERT. You're not my mother.

(And he's out the door after **ELAINE**. **HARRIET**, *meanwhile, pulls on her topcoat.)*

HARRIET. Charlie, what do you do? Rent out the sauna?

CHARLIE. No, no, it's just a family problem.

(POLLY *appears in the courtyard on her way to Charlie's. Through closed curtains, we do not see her clearly.* **CHARLIE** *glances at his watch.)*

Harriet, I apologize to you. Forgetting your Thursday was inexcusable. I'll make it up to you any way I can…

HARRIET. Yeah, but meanwhile, get lost!

(resigned) Well…

(glances in mirror)

HARRIET. *(cont.)* Face it, Harriet. One look in the mirror, I can see I need ironing.

(She throws **CHARLIE** *a kiss, goes.* **POLLY** *knocks on glass door.)*

CHARLIE. Coming!

(Quickly he scurries about putting things in order. Checks his appearance. Turns down lights. And lets **POLLY** *in.)*

(She is a DREAM! Exquisite in gorgeous glittering gown, tasteful jewelry, stylish hairdo. And inwardly she is happy. She has arrived at a decision and is comfortable with it.)

*(***CHARLIE** *and* **POLLY** *are two very beautiful people.)*

CHARLIE. *(holds out his hands for her)* Polly.

POLLY. Charlie.

CHARLIE. *(takes her hands, swings her around a bit)* You look lovely.

POLLY. Thank you, Charlie. You too.

(He gets a flower from the bouquet, gives it to her.)

Thank you. I'm sorry I'm late.

CHARLIE. Actually it worked out for the better. I had a few things to get in order here.

POLLY. *(about the whole scene)* How beautiful you've arranged it all.

CHARLIE. Thank you.

POLLY. *(the cooking)* The famous fourteen-hour sauce.

CHARLIE. The same.

POLLY. *(looks at champagne bottle in bucket)* The Flower Bottle. Of course, what else would it be?

(He smiles.)

Charlie, I have something to say. I'd like to say it right away before I lose my nerve.

CHARLIE. Of course.

POLLY. I've been doing my...little bedtime reading. Interesting, isn't it, how one can live for so many years and still have significant gaps in one's education?

CHARLIE. Yes.

POLLY. Naturally, I did a lot of thinking about the things you've said. About dreams, about fantasies, about fulfilling them. If not now, when? If not now, never. And I realize too what you mean by moving mountains. The biggest mountain of all is yourself. To break out! To try new things! Things you might have been afraid to try before! To bring out the gypsy! To soar, Charlie, to soar!

*(**CHARLIE** says nothing. Listens. He has **POLLY** in the right place, convincing herself.)*

I hope I can soar, Charlie, now that I'm not afraid.

(He smiles. She does too. He clicks on the radio. Soft music fills the room. He holds his arms open for her. She comes forward...to him...)

*(But **POLLY** goes right by him and to the door to the courtyard. Into the room comes **MARC**. **POLLY** goes to **MARC**.)*

*(**CHARLIE** turns to see this. The expectation on his face fades. His chin falls.)*

(simply) I have a confession. Marc isn't my nephew.

MARC. She's not my aunt, either.

*(**CHARLIE***'s mouth is open in utter bewilderment.)*

POLLY. I'm ashamed to admit it, but I was embarrassed about being seen with a younger man.

MARC. Being her nephew, that was my idea.

CHARLIE. *(He's sick.)* Oh, clever. Very clever.

MARC. Thanks. *(gently)* Polly, I'm on the Rome flight, you know.

POLLY. Yes. We'll go to my place.

*(**MARC** nods. She clamps his hand.)*

Let me go first.

MARC. Of course.

(POLLY starts out, stops.)

POLLY. Charlie, I know I don't have to say anything to you about keeping my secret. I don't want Robert to know.

CHARLIE. Oh, no, no.

POLLY. Thank you, Charlie. You're such a dear man.

(She goes. CHARLIE and MARC are alone.)

MARC. *(This is not gloating, but delight that it went well.)* I kept the corners of my mouth up! I stayed confident like you said. Oh, you were so right, you're a genius…

CHARLIE. *(muttering)* A genius…

MARC. Oh, er, Charlie, you're not going to need the champagne now, are you?

CHARLIE. Hmm?…Oh, no, no, take it.

MARC. Thanks. *(Takes bottle. Pause.)* That dinner sure smells good.

CHARLIE. Take it! Take it! Antipasto di la casa! Take it! Take it!…Don't forget the dessert!

MARC. What is it?

CHARLIE. Pear sorbet!

MARC. I love pears!

CHARLIE. Take it! Take it! Take the flowers too! Take the music! Take everything.

(CHARLIE has loaded up MARC who is delighted.)

MARC. Hey, Charlie, thanks! You're the best!

(Out goes MARC. with Charlie's flowers, champagne, whatever he can carry, singing Charlie's Italian song.)

(Alone now, CHARLIE strides across the room in a fury. He crooks his fingers into a gun and aims it at his temple.)

CHARLIE. POW!!!

(black out)

(curtain)

ACT II

Scene One

(The same. A week later. **CHARLIE**, *in stocking feet, stands on an article of furniture, looking out at the beach through binoculars. He doesn't like what he sees.)*

CHARLIE. *(muttering)* Look, look, they're swinging hands like children!…Nuzzling! He's nuzzling her neck right there on the walk!

(at what he sees now) No! Not that!

*(***ROBERT** *sticks his head in the front window.)*

ROBERT. Hi, Charlie. What are you doing?

CHARLIE. Checking the surf to see if anyone is drowning. Looks all right.

*(***CHARLIE**, *obviously in a grouchy mood, steps down.* **ROBERT**, *meanwhile, carrying his attache case, comes in the front door.)*

What do you want, Robert? She's not here.

ROBERT. I know.

CHARLIE. And she hasn't been here, either.

ROBERT. I didn't come to see her. I came to see you. Ever since your birthday dinner for my mother she's been a different person. I've never seen her like this! She's aglow!

*(***CHARLIE** *stifles a growl.)*

Anyway, Charlie, I want to thank you.

CHARLIE. Don't thank me.

ROBERT. Charlie, I'm grateful.

CHARLIE. Don't be grateful.

(CHARLIE is preparing his massage lounge chair and his massage slippers for use.)

ROBERT. Charlie, I'm just trying to say…

CHARLIE. Don't say it.

ROBERT. But you…

CHARLIE. I didn't.

ROBERT. Oh. Oh, I get it. It's better left unsaid.

CHARLIE. You don't get it.

ROBERT. I do, Charlie, I do. Gentlemen don't talk about things like that. Especially to the ladies' son. What man would? He'd be afraid he'd get his face smashed in. Charlie, I'm not going to smash your face in.

CHARLIE. *(dryly)* Thanks.

ROBERT. It's all right with me. If my mother wants to have fun, let her have fun.

CHARLIE. *(wants to end the subject)* All right…

ROBERT. If the father of the woman I care for so much wants to have fun, let him. If they want to have fun together…

CHARLIE. Robert, get off it, will you? Your mother and I are not having an affair.

ROBERT. *(doesn't believe it)* Oh, sure, sure, Charlie. I've got it.

(winks, gives CHARLIE the elbow)

Funny, though. My mother can have a lover and I can't. Doesn't seem fair.

CHARLIE. Go away, Robert. I'm trying to relax.

(CHARLIE has gotten into his lounge chair, slips his feet into his massage slippers.)

ROBERT. I don't know. I've got such a problem.

CHARLIE. Perfect! Approach it as though you were in government. Don't solve it while it's small. Wait for it to get so big it's unsolvable, then you can't be criticized for not being able to solve it.

(CHARLIE turns on slippers massage. Deep into his melancholy, ROBERT hardly seems to notice.)

ROBERT. I'm so low. Where's the sparkle to life? It's not like it was supposed to be. Carol was so beautiful when we got married. So supportive. We were so young, so full of passion and hope. So much in love. With her at my side I was full of confidence. I was going to conquer the business world and live the good life.

(CHARLIE turns up the slippers massage. ROBERT, a man in pain, keeps right on going.)

I'm good at managing money, Charlie. I've got the talent. Not one of my clients has ever gone bankrupt. Not one of my clients has ever gone to jail. A fine here, a fine there, nothing serious.

(CHARLIE turns on the lounge chair massage. Now his whole body vibrates. It doesn't bother ROBERT.)

Carol says it's crass what I do. Crass! *(Now he's getting worked up.)* She hates money, she says! I guess that's why she spends it so fast to get rid of it! Frankly, she'd like to be a radical.

(CHARLIE turns up the massage on the lounge chair. His body vibrates at full speed. ROBERT keeps right on going.)

But she doesn't know what kind to be. All the well-known ones in the Western world are out of fashion. So she's disappointed too. So she's joined the New Age. She's gone into ESP. I'm afraid soon she'll be reading my mind.

(so forlorn) I don't know. My kids ignore me. The dog pees on my leg.

CHARLIE. Robert, I'm relaxing.

ROBERT. Oh, sorry, Charlie, sorry.

(The door buzzer sounds. ROBERT peeks out the front window.)

Elaine! It's Elaine! I don't want her to see me this way, it's so unmacho! I've got to hide!

CHARLIE. *(bounding out of chair)* Don't hide!

ROBERT. The sauna! That's it…

CHARLIE. Not the sauna!

(But **ROBERT** *has already grabbed his attache case and run into the sauna. Meanwhile,* **ELAINE** *has kept buzzing the buzzer.)*

All right, all right, I'm coming.

(He opens the door. **ELAINE** *bursts in, looking chic, of course.)*

ELAINE. He's not here, is he? No! Good! Hi, Poppa.

CHARLIE. Hi.

(goes back to massage chair)

ELAINE. Well, as long as I'm here I should ask you.

CHARLIE. Don't bother. I can live without the question.
(back into his chair)

ELAINE. What's the matter?

CHARLIE. Nothing's the matter.

(turns on massage)

ELAINE. Yes, Poppa, something is. You're different.

CHARLIE. I'm not different!

ELAINE. Everybody here's different. Polly's different, you're different! She's gone up, you've gone down…

CHARLIE. *(bounding out of chair)* I have not gone down!

ELAINE. Yes, Poppa, you have. You growl.

CHARLIE. I do not growl!

ELAINE. You never used to, but you do now. *(imitates his growl)*

CHARLIE. Is that why you came here, to tell me I growl?

ELAINE. *(beginning to weep)* No, Poppa, no…

CHARLIE. *(unaware she is breaking down)* I do not growl! I have not changed! *I* am no different today than I was yesterday! I was no different yesterday than I was the day before…!

ELAINE. Oh, I can't go on this way. I can't! *(breaks down into sobs)*

CHARLIE. *(concerned; embraces her)* Honey, honey…

ELAINE. *(the child)* Oh, Poppa.

CHARLIE. There, there…

ELAINE. I know you'd like to help, Poppa. You always did. Who cleaned my knees when they were skinned? Who comforted me when my date brought me home at ten-thirty and didn't want to sneak up into my room?

CHARLIE. It's George, isn't it, and the periodontist?

ELAINE. No. He gave her up.

CHARLIE. And went back to the endodontist?

ELAINE. *(sniffling)* No. He gave up both of them for golf. Which is worse. Golf takes up twice as much time as a mistress…Oh, why is everything so miserable? I do the right things. I married a man who was going to be a doctor. I have two children, a boy and a girl, in the right order. I have charge accounts in all the right places. I go to charity lunches and buy the raffle tickets. I wear the right clothes. If a new color comes in I'm the first to embrace it. My shoes are pointed even though they hurt like mad. I have the right paintings on the wall even though I don't like looking at them. I'm a reservoir of gossip. Poppa, does everybody get short changed?

(CHARLIE gestures: who knows?)

A successful marriage is a matter of luck, isn't it? Who really knows who you marry? George and I were so much in love. Now he pays no attention to me. It seems as though we're enemies. I don't want him as an enemy.

CHARLIE. Of course not. Who needs enemies? We have our own selves. That's enemy enough.

ELAINE. I must be older, Poppa. I'm getting philosophical myself.

(He smiles.)

Poppa, do you have to be a senior to move mountains?

CHARLIE. *(This is serious talk.)* No, of course not. But you do have to stop worrying about what people will think.

ELAINE. Maybe I should be more receptive to Robert's advances. Maybe I should stop calling him names and listen at least to what he has to say.

*(**ROBERT** pops out of sauna, dripping wet, holding his attaché case, of course.)*

ROBERT. I heard you! Elaine, it's wonderful! At least you give me hope!

(moves to her)

I will make a fuss over you. It will be so easy, you are so lovely.

*(**ELAINE** likes this. She is mesmerized.)*

We will spend the day together. We will go to tea at the Bel Air Hotel. We will sit by the running brook and look at the swans. I will touch your fingertips so lightly and send little waves of electricity through your body…

(phone in his attaché case rings)

Excuse me.

(puts down attaché case, opens it, answers phone) Hello!

ELAINE. *(spell broken)* Oh, the man's impossible.

(exits in a huff)

ROBERT. *(to **ELAINE**)* Wait!

*(into phone as he runs after **ELAINE**)*

48% international, 36% U.S. growth, 16% money market…Oh, in that case 55% money market, 29% international, 16% U.S. growth…

(He's gone.)

*(**POLLY** sticks her head in from the courtyard.)*

POLLY. They're gone! Good!

*(**POLLY** comes in. Her spirits are high. She wears a Hawaiian skirt and a lei around her neck.)*

POLLY. *(cont.)* Look what I just bought!

(twirls, showing off her skirt)

Marc and I went shopping in the mall. We may be going to Hawaii.

*(**MARC** comes in. His spirits are high. He wears a Hawaiian shirt and holds a ukelele.)*

MARC. Hi, Charlie!

CHARLIE. *(dully)* Hi.

*(**MARC** begins to strum the ukelele, singing a Hawaiian song. He doesn't know the words, so he makes up sounds.)*

MARC. Haka haka, muka muka! Haka haka, muka muka!

*(**CHARLIE** growls. **POLLY** goes into her version of the Hawaiian hula.)*

POLLY. Look what I learned, Charlie!

(She does the appropriate hand movements as she explains their meaning.)

This is wind…This is rain…This is moon.

MARC. Isn't she great, Charlie?

*(He keeps strumming and singing as **POLLY** keeps at it.)*

POLLY. This is boy…This is girl… This is love.

MARC. Love, Charlie, that's love!

*(**CHARLIE** growls. By now we realize that **CHARLIE** has an assortment of growls. Finally, **POLLY** stops, out of breath.)*

Hey, maybe we'll go to Saudi Arabia some day! You can do that with seven veils!

POLLY. No, thank you. Not without a respirator!

*(**POLLY** and **MARC** laugh together. **CHARLIE**, on the outside, growls.)*

You can't tell by looking at me now, but I was a dancer. Before motherhood, before marriage, before. Just something else that slipped away…Charlie, I feel very good.

(She brushes **MARC**'s *hair back off his forehead, much as a mother does with a child.)*

MARC. Me, too! Charlie, how're you doing with your new girlfriend?

CHARLIE. Oh, fine, fine.

*(***POLLY*** drops his hand. This is the first she's heard of "Charlie's new girlfriend." Though controlled, she can show jealousy as well as* **CHARLIE**.*)*

POLLY. Charlie, I didn't know you had a new girlfriend.

MARC. *(ever helpful)* Oh, sure! I told him about you, he told me about her! Charlie's in love!

POLLY. Really?

MARC. Hey, maybe we can double-date someday, the four of us!

CHARLIE. Marc, don't you have to go fly an airplane or something?

MARC. As a matter of fact, I do. Polly, I've got to be going.

POLLY. I know. I'll walk you to the car.

MARC. Great!

*(***POLLY*** exits first.* **MARC** *holds back a bit. Sotto:)*

You're a genius, all right. Look, a smile on my face and a bounce to my step…Oh, Charlie, thanks for the book you gave Polly for her birthday. Page 98. Wow.

*(***MARC*** exits. Frustrated, angry,* **CHARLIE** *growls. He moves around, kicking things. Gets binoculars, looks out window after* **POLLY** *and* **MARC**.*)*

CHARLIE. Look, look at that!…Look at them!

(Phone rings. He grabs it.)

Yeah!…Oh, hi, Sam…Sam, I'm kind of busy now.

(not too enthusiastic) Sam, that's great…Sam, that's terrific…Sam, I'm glad you passed it, but I've got something important going on right now!…All right, I'll call you and I'm sorry I was sharp. Who needs a kidney stone anyway?

(Hangs up. Looks through the binoculars again at **POLLY** *and* **MARC**. *Growls. Then:)*

CHARLIE. *(cont.)* Aw, who cares? Who cares? There are women all over the place!

(looks again)

(Sees **POLLY** *returning. Hides binoculars, goes to his office area, gets busy folding circulars as though he doesn't care.* **POLLY** *returns.)*

POLLY. He's a very nice young man.

CHARLIE. Oh, yeah.

*(****CHARLIE****, of course, doesn't want* **POLLY** *to know he's jealous.)*

POLLY. Confused, though. Like everybody else. Does he want to stay with the airlines? Does he want to settle down? What does he really want?

CHARLIE. Polly, there are a million envelopes to get out.

POLLY. Oh, sure.

(She will join him at the work, folding circulars and subsequently stuffing envelopes.)

Anyway, I want to thank you for being such a good friend and keeping my confidence. I'm not ready for Robert to know about Marc yet.

CHARLIE. He knows you have a lover.

POLLY. *(surprised)* He does?

CHARLIE. He thinks it's me.

POLLY. You??!!

CHARLIE. Yeah, isn't that hilarious!

(growls; about circulars)

One orange one, one green one into each envelope.

POLLY. I know, Charlie!

(She complies.) So…tell me about her.

CHARLIE. Who?

POLLY. Your new girlfriend.

CHARLIE. Who? Oh, her.

POLLY. Marc thinks this one is special.

    (fishing) Is she, Charlie? Is she special?

CHARLIE. *(firmly)* Yes, yes, she is!

    (Charlie's positiveness brings out a bit more jealousy in **POLLY**.)

POLLY. She's very pretty, I suppose.

CHARLIE. Oh, yes.

POLLY. Smart. She understands the things you say.

CHARLIE. Oh, sure.

POLLY. Sensitive, compassionate, very female…in the best way?

CHARLIE. Absolutely.

POLLY. And she likes a lot of the things you like?

CHARLIE. Most of them.

POLLY. Perhaps I'll get to meet her someday. What's her name?

CHARLIE. Hmm?

POLLY. Her name.

CHARLIE. Oh, her name.

POLLY. Look, you don't have to tell me if you don't want to! Keep it a secret!

CHARLIE. Sarah.

POLLY. Sarah? I don't know her then, do I? Well, that's a very nice name and I'm sure she brings out the gypsy in you.

CHARLIE. Of course! Of course!

    (offers wet sponge)

    Here, wet the backs of the envelopes…

    (Polly's jealousy has made her testy.)

POLLY. Charlie, I'm sixty-two years old! I know how to wet the backs of envelopes with a sponge and seal them!

CHARLIE. *(testy too)* All right, all right.

POLLY. My father used to tell me how to do things and I did them just as he said. My husband used to tell me how to do things and I did them just as he said. Now I'm not going to let anybody tell me what to do anymore.

(a request) Tell me what to do, Charlie.

CHARLIE. I'm not going to tell you what to do.

POLLY. *(emphatically)* Go on, tell me!

CHARLIE. No!

POLLY. *(demanding)* Tell me!

CHARLIE. All right, all right! Here's what I want you to do…

POLLY. I won't do it! I'm not going to do something just because someone tells me to do it…!

CHARLIE. All right, all right!

POLLY. I'm not arguing with you, Charlie, but I am practicing.

CHARLIE. Oh.

(They continue folding circulars, stuffing the envelopes.)

POLLY. I also don't want you to embarrass me about Marc because he's younger than I am.

(touch of sarcasm) I don't have your experience. With young or old. But I had this little fantasy. Why do people have fantasies? Why do some women want to be made love to by left-handed men?

CHARLIE. They do?

POLLY. I don't know. I'm just using that as an illustration. So I had this silly little thing about being made love to by a younger man in a flight officer's uniform. Don't ask me why. Maybe it had something to do with Ralph and his airline stewardesses. But I don't think it's any more bizarre than wanting to be made love to in a haystack or by a stranger with a droopy moustache.

CHARLIE. I never heard of that one.

POLLY. You talked about living out dreams, fulfilling fantasies, if not now, when?

CHARLIE. I get it! It's all my fault!

POLLY. Oh, Charlie, I'm not talking fault. This is much more important than fault. I learned something about myself. I learned I'm not as timid as I've always believed. Frankly, I'm surprised I was able to do it. More than surprised. Pleased. Pleased that I could and still feel comfortable with myself. Even more than comfortable. Elated. So don't try to embarrass me…

CHARLIE. *(not happy at all)* All right, all right!

(Door buzzer buzzes. Angrily, CHARLIE flings open the door.)

Yeah!

(Outside is a kid whom we don't see who says something to CHARLIE which we don't hear. Then:)

I'm sorry, Billy, I can't come out and play Frisbees.

(He shuts the door. They go back to work on the circulars and envelopes. But CHARLIE's jealousy is working overtime. He seethes.)

POLLY. *(at length)* What's the matter now?

CHARLIE. Nothing, nothing!

POLLY. Oh, it's something.

CHARLIE. You didn't have to give him the book!

POLLY. What book?

(CHARLIE gives up all pretense of working, bounces up.)

CHARLIE. *Our* book!

POLLY. Oh.

(simply) We don't have a book.

CHARLIE. The one I gave you.

POLLY. Yes, you gave it to me. So it's *my* book. It is not *our* book. And I can do what I want with my book.

CHARLIE. Oh, the hell with the book! He's out there, mauling you on the street!

POLLY. He is not mauling me…

CHARLIE. In front of everybody to see!

POLLY. I thought you didn't care about what people think!

CHARLIE. I don't!

POLLY. Charlie, you don't own me. I can do whatever I want. In front of people or not.

CHARLIE. Oh, I know that, but I thought something was developing between us that was special and unique.

POLLY. You thought something was developing between us that was so special and unique that you've developed it with an untold number of other women.

CHARLIE. That is not exactly accurate.

POLLY. Then what is exactly accurate?

CHARLIE. Well…

POLLY. And while you're figuring that out *(her jealousy)* you can also tell me what's so special and unique about her!

CHARLIE. *(puzzled)* Who?

POLLY. Sarah!

CHARLIE. Who's Sarah?

POLLY. You told me!

CHARLIE. Oh, *that* Sarah!

POLLY. Yes, *that* Sarah.

CHARLIE. You're jealous.

POLLY. I am not!

CHARLIE. There is no Sarah! What I mean is, there is a Sarah, but she's Polly!

POLLY. I'm Polly!

CHARLIE. Yes, you're Sarah!

(Pause. Then:)

POLLY. Charlie, I think we've been arguing like teenagers. For a moment, let's slow down.

CHARLIE. All right.

POLLY. You're saying you're in love with Sarah who really is me?

CHARLIE. *(that goes a step too far)* Did I say "love"? I said…

POLLY. Don't go all the way out on a limb, Charlie, but do inch yourself along a bit.

CHARLIE. Yes, I admit to a certain feeling.

POLLY. Special and unique?

CHARLIE. Yes.

POLLY. About me?

CHARLIE. Of course, about you! Who else are we talking about?!

POLLY. Well, that part is nice, but Charlie, I'm not sure the things you say are really the truth. Frankly, I wonder if you know yourself.

CHARLIE. I know, I know!

POLLY. Well then, I admit to a…certain feeling about you.

CHARLIE. *(puzzled)* Then why…?

POLLY. *(This is serious.)* But I'm beginning to get a very funny idea about you. I'm beginning to see something I didn't see before. You say to me, "You are a free person, move a mountain." But when I do, you grumble.

Tell me. If you didn't have that special and unique feeling about a person, she could do as she pleased? It wouldn't matter which mountain she moved, would it?

CHARLIE. No, I suppose not…

POLLY. But because of this special and unique feeling that person better be careful. If she picked learning Japanese, reading all of Proust, sky-diving even, it would be all right.

CHARLIE. Those are very good mountains!

POLLY. But not being made love to by a left-handed man? I use that as an illustration.

CHARLIE. *(Her logic is driving him wild.)* I know what you're doing!

POLLY. So it's you who passes judgment on the mountain she wishes to move…

CHARLIE. What man in the world wants his girl to be unfaithful to him?!

POLLY. *(exploding)* How can I be unfaithful to you when I've never been faithful to you?!

CHARLIE. *(knows he's in trouble; wants to change the subject)* I think we should do another pasta test…

POLLY. I don't need another pasta test! Charlie, I'm not your girl, nor have I ever been!

CHARLIE. Well, I was just using that as an illustration…

POLLY. And if I were! If! What then? Suddenly you become proprietary? Suddenly you become judgmental? Charlie, is that why Grace left you?

CHARLIE. Grace was not interested in left-handed men…

POLLY. I am not talking about that now! I am talking about *everything!* Were you the Big Rooster in the coop? Did you have to give your stamp of approval? How many times did you tell her to wet the sponge and seal the envelopes…?

CHARLIE. Will you please stop with the sponge and envelopes…?

POLLY. You know what, Charlie? You're a skimmer. You can scrape the icing off the cake. But you can't handle the nitty-gritty. You can't take the person as she really is. You are a fake and a fraud. You better move your own mountain!

CHARLIE. My mountain is perfectly all right, thank you!

POLLY. I don't know where we have to go together, if anywhere, but as of now I will have as many nephews visiting me as I please!

CHARLIE. Yeah! Yeah! Well, if you can have as many nephews visiting you as you please, I can have as many nieces visiting me!

POLLY. Agreed! Goodbye, Charlie!

(She exits, slamming the door. He flings open the door and shouts after her.)

CHARLIE. Goodbye, Polly!

(He slams the door. Seethes. Then he opens it again and:)

Hey, Billy, don't go away! I'll be right out with my Frisbee!

(blackout)

Scene Two

(The same as Act I, Scene 1. Blinds closed, shutting out the afternoon sun. **CHARLIE** *and* **GWEN** *are into their gypsy dance, he with flourishes, she indifferently.)*

CHARLIE. Zigeuner!…Zigeuner!

(He does some wild flourishing around the room).

Zigeuner!…Zigeuner!…Come on, say "zigeuner."

GWEN. *(without spirit)* Zigeuner.

CHARLIE. No, not like that. Give it some feeling! *(flourishes about)*

GWEN. *(tries)* Zigeuner…Zigeuner…

CHARLIE. *(urging her)* More, more.

GWEN. *(tries again)* Zigeuner…Zigeuner.

CHARLIE. No, no, that's so fake!

GWEN. I'm trying!

CHARLIE. Try harder!

GWEN. I'm trying as hard as I can!
(giving up entirely) It's no use. I can't.

CHARLIE. You can! You always could!…More wine!

GWEN. I don't want more wine. I'm acidy as it is.

CHARLIE. You never got acidy before. You could drink by the barrel!

GWEN. That was before, this is now.

CHARLIE. What do you mean?

GWEN. You know what I mean.

CHARLIE. No, I do not! "That was before, this is now." Is it a riddle?

GWEN. Charlie, we've always been honest with each other.

CHARLIE. Of course.

GWEN. That's why it worked so well. We both knew what it was. Nothing more, nothing less. It was enough.

CHARLIE. It still is!

GWEN. No, it's different now.

CHARLIE. What's different?

GWEN. You are.

CHARLIE. I'm not different!

GWEN. Yes, you are. Very much so. Before you were neutral. I was neutral; you were neutral. Now you're not neutral anymore.

CHARLIE. I'm neutral!

GWEN. *(This is not jealousy.)* Not since Polly.

CHARLIE. She has nothing to do with this!

GWEN. Yes, she does. You're in love, Charlie. That moves you off neutral.

CHARLIE. I'm on neutral!

GWEN. Now it would be all mixed up with other things. With anger. With you wanting to get back at her. It's no longer pure.

CHARLIE. It's pure!

(door buzzer sounds)

GWEN. *(alarmed)* Someone's coming! I've got to hide!

CHARLIE. You don't have to hide! We're not doing anything! I'm not neutral, remember!

GWEN. The sauna!

CHARLIE. Not the sauna!

(But she starts for the sauna as door buzzer keeps buzzing.)

All right, all right, I'm coming!

(CHARLIE opens the door. In comes HARRIET, singing.)

HARRIET. "Mine eyes have seen the glory of the coming of the Lord…"

CHARLIE. Harriet!

GWEN. *(has not quite gotten into the sauna)* Harriet!

HARRIET. Oh, hi, Gwen.

CHARLIE. You know each other?

HARRIET. Oh, sure. Gweh, have you noticed? Charlie's not on neutral anymore.

GWEN. I was just telling him that!

HARRIET. That's it, Charlie! You're finished!

(She gives him the trashy lingeree.) Here! Put it in your scrapbook!

(Starts out. Looks in mirror.)

Yeah. I'm a wreck all right. I'll never live to be as old as I look…Goodbye, Charlie, goodbye forever!

(She goes.)

GWEN. You see. All your lady friends know it. You're not on neutral anymore. They're all gone…

CHARLIE. I'm neutral, I'm neutral…!

(door buzzer sounds)

GWEN. Someone's coming! I have to hide!

CHARLIE. You don't have to hide!

(but she's already bolting into the sauna)

Not the sauna!

(but she's already in it, as the buzzer keeps buzzing)

All right, all right!

*(**CHARLIE** opens door. **ROBERT**, carrying attache case, bursts in, looks around.)*

ROBERT. Are you alone?…Anyone in the sauna?

CHARLIE. *(wants him out)* Robert…

ROBERT. *(insistent)* Elaine! Is Elaine in the sauna?!

CHARLIE. Elaine is not in the sauna!!

ROBERT. Good! I've got to talk to you.

CHARLIE. I can't talk now. I'm busy getting off neutral. Go away.

ROBERT. Elaine finally agreed to spend an evening with me. Last night. I couldn't believe my good fortune!

*(**CHARLIE**'s shoulders sag. **ROBERT** is going to tell him about it whether he wants to know or not.)*

CHARLIE. Robert, I don't need this.

ROBERT. I made arrangements for a suite at the hotel; corporate connection. I filled the rooms with flowers; discounted by Flower Fair; I do their pension program. Music with a Latin beat. Salsa. Everyone's making love to it these days. Dinner up from the restaurant. Candlelight. Champagne. Eyes meeting flirtingly. A touch here, a touch there. She was melting…came the moment, I couldn't.

CHARLIE. You couldn't?

ROBERT. *(This is very painful.)* I could not make love to the wife of a man with whom I was in a limited partnership.

CHARLIE. I see.

ROBERT. *(total dismay)* Advise me! What am I to do?

CHARLIE. Castration.

ROBERT. What?!

CHARLIE. You don't need it anymore.

ROBERT. *(desperate)* What are you saying?!

CHARLIE. Robert, when a woman finally puts aside her inhibitions and says "yes," and the man who has been urging her to say "yes," says "no," forget it. It will never ever be. From that moment on she will not even know you exist.

ROBERT. That's terrible!

CHARLIE. So while you're still intact, go home. Take your wife to the hotel suite. Or a neighbor. But please get out of here.

(back to his computer)

I have something important to do.

*(The phone in **ROBERT**'s attache case rings.)*

ROBERT. The door buzzer!

CHARLIE. It's your phone!

ROBERT. Someone's coming!

CHARLIE. No one's coming!

ROBERT. I've got to hide.

CHARLIE. Don't hide! Answer the phone!

ROBERT. The sauna!

CHARLIE. Not the sauna!

(But **ROBERT** *has already bolted into the sauna…* **CHARLIE** *watches. A beat.* **GWEN** *screams, comes bolting out of the sauna.)*

GWEN. Charlie, you knew I was hiding in there! Why did you let a strange man come in on me?

*(***CHARLIE** *is about to say something, but* **ROBERT** *comes rushing out of the sauna.)*

ROBERT. *(puzzled)* Charlie, why are you hiding a woman with her clothes on in your sauna?

*(***CHARLIE** *is about to answer, but:)*

GWEN. That, young man, is none of your business!

CHARLIE. Gwen…!

GWEN. As for you, Charlie, from now on whether my clothes are on or off is no business of yours either!
(at door) Goodbye, Charlie, goodbye forever!

(goes)

ROBERT. *(to* **CHARLIE***)* This is very odd, Charlie. Do you often hide women with clothes on in your sauna?

CHARLIE. No, I…

ROBERT. Did you hide my mother with her clothes on in your sauna?

CHARLIE. I did not hide your mother…

ROBERT. Maybe you did and forgot! Charlie, are you getting old and eccentric?

CHARLIE. I am not old and eccentric!

ROBERT. *(referring to* **GWEN***)* I should run after her and apologize for you.

CHARLIE. I have nothing to apologize for!

ROBERT. True. Being old and eccentric is not your fault.

CHARLIE. *(getting furious)* I am not old and eccentric! I am…!

ROBERT. Excuse me, Charlie. I'm-going to do just that.

(starts out)

Madame, I must apologize for the old and eccentric…

(is gone)

CHARLIE. *(fuming)* Don't call me old and eccentric! I am not…!

(realizes **ROBERT** *left his attache case)*

Wait! Your attache case.

(But by now **ROBERT** *is gone.* **CHARLIE** *is ready to fling the attache case out after* **ROBERT***, but the phone in the attache case rings.* **CHARLIE** *rips open the case, barks into phone.)*

Yeah!…

(a glance out toward the departed **ROBERT** *)*

SELL…SELL EVERYTHING!

(He slams down phone.)

(blackout)

Scene Three

(The same. A few days later. The middle of the afternoon. **ELAINE** *is discovered, pacing up and down, worried. After a moment she calls at the bathroom door.)*

ELAINE. Poppa.

(no answer from within.) Poppa, are you all right?

(still no answer) Poppa, please answer me…

(Bathroom door opens. Out comes **CHARLIE** *wearing a robe over light pants. He is far different than we have seen him before. His hair is disheveled. He walks laboriously, hunched and spiritless. Also, he feels sorry for himself.)*

Poppa, are you feeling better?

CHARLIE. Shhh. Not so loud.

ELAINE. *(quietly)* Poppa, are you feeling better?

CHARLIE. *(sound of pain)* Ich.

ELAINE. What hurts?

CHARLIE. What doesn't? Even my hair. I need an anesthetic just to comb it.

ELAINE. *(reaching for him)* Poppa…

CHARLIE. *(alarm)* Don't touch'me!

(She doesn't.)

I'm turning to powder.

(He pats himself on the shoulder. Sure enough, powder rises.)

*(***ELAINE** *knows* **CHARLIE** *is exaggerating. Still, how to handle this?* **CHARLIE** *crosses to his chair and very carefully lowers himself into it. Emits a big sigh.)*

ELAINE. Turn on the chair! Give yourself a nice massage!

CHARLIE. The jiggling makes me nauseous.

ELAINE. *(an idea)* I'll fix you a cup of tea! Red Zinger! You like that…

CHARLIE. If you wish.

ELAINE. Not if I wish, Poppa, it's if you wish.

CHARLIE. If you wish, I wish. If you don't wish, I don't wish. I can't decide. My brain is melting.

ELAINE. I've got a marvelous idea! I'll go to the Boulangerie, get some roast chicken and fruit salad. We'll go down to the ocean and have a picnic.

CHARLIE. Too many sand fleas.

ELAINE. We'll go to the park instead.

CHARLIE. Too many grass fleas.

ELAINE. The gardens! We'll sit right in the middle of the flowers!

CHARLIE. Too many bumblebees.

(Her shoulders sag. Nothing is working.)

Elaine, you've got a million things to do. Go do them. That's better than sitting here with me.

(big sigh)

ELAINE. Poppa, I want to help.

CHARLIE. I'm fine, fine.

ELAINE. No, you're not.

CHARLIE. I'll just lean back, rest, and try not to get gout in either foot.

ELAINE. Let's put some music on! You love opera!
(has moved to albums) Verdi!

CHARLIE. Too melancholy.

ELAINE. Puccini!

CHARLIE. Too melodic.

ELAINE. Offenbach!

CHARLIE. Too charming.

ELAINE. Poppa, I'm going to call George and tell him to come over.

CHARLIE. Yes, that's what I need, a doctor.

ELAINE. Good!

(goes to phone)

CHARLIE. Call the paramedics. Tell them not to bring a stretcher, bring a slab instead.

ELAINE. *(has had enough of this)* Poppa, you've got to stop this! This is not real for you!

CHARLIE. *(shrugs)* What's real?

ELAINE. Real is your fire, your zip, your spirit…

> *(CHARLIE rises. Slowly, laboriously he exits through the kitchen door to service porch in rear as ELAINE goes on.)*

Your insults, your refusal to complain, your ability to look at the bright side…

> *(But CHARLIE is gone. Her shoulders sag. What to do? Front door opens. ROBERT sticks his head in.)*

ROBERT. *(cheerfully)* Hi!

ELAINE. You!

> *(This is a new ROBERT. A man full of confidence and sense of worth. Big smile. Carries his attache case)*

Please don't start that again. As far as I'm concerned you don't exist.

ROBERT. *(cheerfully)* I know. Charlie told me I wouldn't. But that's not what I've come to talk about.

> *(ELAINE will realize she is looking at a totally different ROBERT.)*

ROBERT. Have you seen what has happened to the stock market?

ELAINE. No, I never pay attention.

ROBERT. Dropped! Like a stone! Millions have been lost! Millions!

ELAINE. Oh.

ROBERT. Don't say "oh" like that.

> *(eager to tell her)* When I got to the office the other day I discovered that my assistant, on phone orders from me, had sold out all stock positions! Mine, my clients', yours and George's too! Everything!

ELAINE. So?

ROBERT. So it was the most brilliant move a financial planner could do! Sell before the drop! I'm being called a genius! Money Magazine will do a feature on me! Louis Rukeyser wants me on Wall Street Week! I'm being deluged with people begging me to manage their money!

ELAINE. Robert, that's wonderful…!

ROBERT. And the thing is I don't even remember giving my assistant that order!

(CHARLIE, paying no attention to ROBERT and ELAINE, paddles back in. Holds an ice bag. Settles back in his chair, applies ice bag to his head.)

…What does that mean?

ELAINE. I don't know.

ROBERT. That I did it without even knowing what I did!… What does that mean?

ELAINE. I have no idea.

ROBERT. That I have an internal mechanism which enables me to sense major movements in the market! And when that happens my unconscious takes over and issues orders I don't even know about!

ELAINE. Tell me!

ROBERT. That from now on you can expect from me even more genius things!

ELAINE. I can hardly wait!

ROBERT. Look at me! A new man! My chest has expanded! My chin thrusts out! My stride is strong!

ELAINE. I can see it!

(Phone in Robert's attache case has rung.)

ROBERT. Excuse me.

(opens case, answers phone)

Yes!…Ah, yes, I've been waiting for your call!…Yes… yes…yes! Good! It's a done deal! Shake hands on it! *(shakes hands over the phone)* Good!

(hangs up) That was George.

ELAINE. My husband?

ROBERT. I just sold him my interest in our limited partnership, so I no longer have any compunction about
making love to his wife…*That* is my latest genius thing.

ELAINE. *(impressed)* My, suddenly you have taken shape.

ROBERT. Thank you.

> *(Ignored too long,* **CHARLIE** *emits the most awful chok-
ing sound. Which draws* **ELAINE***'s and* **ROBERT***'s
attention.)*

ROBERT. *(cont.)* Charlie, I didn't see you sitting there!

CHARLIE. I know.

ROBERT. *(genuinely concerned)* What's the matter?

ELAINE. *(dryly)* He's turning to powder.

> *(To demonstrate,* **CHARLIE** *pats his shoulder. More
powder.)*

> *(to* **ROBERT***)* Love! I knew I'd have love trouble with my
teenage son. I didn't think I would with my teenage
father.

ROBERT. *(crossing to* **CHARLIE***)* This is terrible! I hate seeing
you this way.

CHARLIE. Yes, it's sad.

ROBERT. *(firmly)* Charlie, I'm a new man! Poised, self-confi-
dent, seething with self-worth, as you knew I could be!
I am going to help you!

> *(pause)* But not right now. Elaine comes first.

ELAINE. I like that.

ROBERT. I can't help myself. I have this internal mechanism that drives my behavior.

ELAINE. Yes, I certainly have to take that into account.

ROBERT. *(moving to her)* Forget the hotel. We'll start anew.
There is this country inn buried in the trees. Music
comes down from speakers hidden in the branches.
Vivaldi. Rachmaninov…

ELAINE. Will you still touch my fingertips so lightly?

ROBERT. Of course.

ELAINE. Both hands?

ROBERT. And the hairline on your forehead.

(Phone rings in Robert's attache case. He answers.)

Hello…What?

*(to **ELAINE**)* Your husband.

ELAINE. George?

(takes phone) George.

*(Listens. Then covers phone. To **ROBERT**:)*

He knows!

ROBERT. How can he know?

ELAINE. He's a doctor, he knows everything!

(back to phone) Yes…Yes…Yes.

(tone changes) George…

(melting) George…George…Right away.

(hangs up) I'm going home.

ROBERT. What?!

ELAINE. He's giving up his golf game to take me to lunch. That French place. That's love!

(excited) Maybe we can get back to what it was before! We have to try!

*(Crosses to **CHARLIE** who has been paying no attention to them.)*

Goodbye, Poppa. I have to go.

(kisses him)

ROBERT. Wait! What about me?

*(**ELAINE** exits. **ROBERT** grabs his attache case, runs after her as:)*

What about my internal mechanism? Wait! We have to talk some more…!

*(**ROBERT**'s gone. **CHARLIE** is alone. Now, "painfully," he rises, carries ice bag, disappears into back of the condo.)*

(POLLY comes in. She, too, is experiencing total depression. In fact, she has reverted to her earlier self. Dowdily dressed, she schleps to Charlie's phone, makes a call.)

POLLY. Hello, this is Polly Adamson…Yes, I know you couldn't reach me. My phone's already been disconnected. I just want to be sure you're coming…Fine. I'll be waiting.

(She hangs up, leaves a coin and exits.)

(CHARLIE reappears, walking with a cane, crosses to bathroom, exits into it.)

(POLLY reenters, returning books which she puts on a shelf, exits.)

(CHARLIE reappears with cane and hot water bottle… does not see POLLY reenter carrying huge plant. She crosses to where she will put plant down, and by then CHARLIE sees her.)

CHARLIE. What is this?

POLLY. I'm returning your plant.

CHARLIE. I don't mean that. I mean this.

(emulates her schlepping)

POLLY. You're doing it too.

(emulates his schlepping)

CHARLIE. You're right! I despise people who feel sorry for themselves! That includes me!

(He tosses his cane aside, takes off robe, puts on a bright shirt.)

There!

(Now she turns and starts out.)

Where are you going?

POLLY. I've got things to do.

(By now CHARLIE spots the coin POLLY left by his telephone.)

CHARLIE. What's this? You made a phone call? Why did you make a call on my phone when you've got one of your own?

POLLY. I'd rather not say.

(turns to leave)

CHARLIE. Wait! Something funny's going on.

POLLY. My phone is disconnected. That's why I used your phone.

CHARLIE. Why is it disconnected?

POLLY. I'd rather not say.

CHARLIE. You've got to say!

(It becomes apparent now, but not immediately to **CHAR-LIE***, that* **POLLY** *is fighting back tears.)*

POLLY. It's what a person usually does when a person moves.

CHARLIE. Who's moving?

POLLY. I am.

CHARLIE. *(stunned)* Why are you moving?

POLLY. I've decided I don't like it here.

CHARLIE. Since when?

POLLY. Since I decided.

CHARLIE. Why don't you like it here?

POLLY. I'd rather not say.

CHARLIE. Damn it! Double damn it!! You can't keep saying "I'd rather not say"!

POLLY. I can do whatever I want!

CHARLIE. *(doesn't want to get into that again)* All right, all right, but…

POLLY. *(her tears more evident now)* Charlie, will you please stop badgering me!

CHARLIE. I'm not badgering you! I'm just trying to find out…

POLLY. One more question and I'm going to scream!

CHARLIE. But at least tell me…

*(***POLLY** *screams.)*

I just want to know…

*(***POLLY** *screams again.)*

I'm only…

(**POLLY** *screams again.*)

Keep that up, we'll have the police knocking down the front door!

POLLY. *(collecting herself somewhat)* I'm sorry. I apologize. I feel better now.

CHARLIE. I wish I did! I don't know anything more about what's going on than I did before!

(door buzzer sounds)

Go away! Nobody's here!

(But **POLLY**, *fairly certain she knows who is there, opens the door.* **MARC** *comes in.)*

Oh, it's you.

MARC. Hi, Charlie.

(A significant look passes between **MARC** *and* **POLLY** *which* **CHARLIE** *does not catch.)*

CHARLIE. Do you know anything about this?

MARC. What?

CHARLIE. Polly's leaving.

MARC. No. I just came by to say goodbye.

CHARLIE. All right, goodbye. Have a nice flight wherever you're going.

MARC. I didn't mean goodbye for just now. I mean goodbye. I'm not coming back.

CHARLIE. What? Oh, that's why Polly's going? You two are going off together. Is that it?

*(***ELAINE*** comes running in through the door by which she left, crosses, exits far door…as everyone looks at her. Now* **ROBERT**, *still holding his attaché case, comes running in looking for her.)*

ROBERT. She came through here! I saw her! Where is she?…The sauna!

CHARLIE. She's not in the sauna!

(points in the direction **ELAINE** *went)* That way!

(But by now **ROBERT** *has seen* **MARC**, *is puzzled.)*

ROBERT. Who is he?

CHARLIE. He used to be your cousin, now it seems he's going to be your father.

ROBERT. How can he be my father? He's younger than I am.

CHARLIE. It doesn't matter! The world doesn't run by truth, but by belief! If you believe he is your father, that's enough!

*(***ELAINE*** peeks her head in at the door she has run out of. She sees* **ROBERT**…*Yelps! Vanishes.* **ROBERT** *has seen her.)*

ROBERT. Elaine!

(He runs after her and out.)

CHARLIE. Poor kids. I guess they're just going to have to thrash around a few more years yet. *(back to* **MARC** *and* **POLLY**, *grimly)* So, you two are going off together…I'm not surprised.

POLLY. No, Charlie. Marc's going one way, I'm going another.

CHARLIE. *(puzzled)* But…

MARC. Yes. I want to thank you for everything, Charlie…

(suddenly it comes to **CHARLIE***)*

CHARLIE. Wait a minute, wait a minute!…I get it! You dumped her!

POLLY. *(wanting to mollify)* Charlie…

*(***CHARLIE*** flies into a rage.)*

CHARLIE. That's it, isn't it? You dumped her! You got what you wanted out of it, then you dumped her!

*(***MARC*** can hardly say anything into* **CHARLIE**'s *fury.)*

POLLY. *(still trying to calm things)* Charlie, please…

CHARLIE. *(won't be stopped)* No, no, absolutely not!…Who do you think you are?!

(CHARLIE has gotten pugnacious! Begins to poke cane at MARC, driving him backwards.)

MARC. Charlie, what are you doing…?!

POLLY. *(pleading)* Charlie…!

(But CHARLIE keeps after MARC with the cane, poking at him. MARC keeps falling back.)

CHARLIE. …What makes you think you can trifle with a person's feelings, then just toss her aside?!

MARC. Charlie, don't do that…"

POLLY. Charlie, stop it…!

(But there's no stopping him.)

CHARLIE. Where's your sense of decency? *I* don't see decency in you! I don't see loyalty! I don't see respect! What do I see? Self-centeredness! Me, me, me!

POLLY. Charlie, you're going crazy!

CHARLIE. *He's* crazy if he thinks he can get away with it! There's a word for guys like you! Rats!

(MARC doesn't want to fight back. Retreats as CHARLIE keeps after him with the cane.)

You should worship the ground she walks on! You should kiss the hem of her dress! You should thank your lucky stars she'd even give you a passing glance! Any man would bust a gut to have her! Grace, charm, sensitivity, depth of feeling! One of a kind! The quintessential woman! I will not let you hurt her!

POLLY. *(interjecting)* Charlie, it's no good between Marc and me!

CHARLIE. It is! You were happy! I wasn't happy, but you were happy! You danced the hula, you laughed, you moved mountains…!

POLLY. It was all fantasy!

CHARLIE. No!

POLLY. I cannot give him what he wants!

CHARLIE. You can!

POLLY. He wants to get married!

CHARLIE. So?

POLLY. He wants to have children of his own!

(He starts to say something, but of course he is stuck. The mood changes.)

He has a life to start, I have one to end! When he's forty, I'll be seventy; when he's fifty, I'll be eighty; when he's sixty – vigorous like you – I'll be powder! He will want me not to grow older while he does. I don't see how I can manage it.

*(**CHARLIE** is nodding his head.)*

CHARLIE. Reality once again.

POLLY. It's bigger than we are, Charlie, no matter what we may think.

CHARLIE. *(to **MARC**)* I'm sorry I pummeled you. You are a nice young man. *(Pats him.)*

MARC. Thank you, Charlie. Everything you say about Polly is true.

*(to **POLLY**)* No matter what, I'm not going to forget you.

POLLY. Thank you, dear. Good luck.

MARC. 'Bye, Charlie. I'm not going to forget you either.

*(**CHARLIE** smiles. **MARC** goes. **CHARLIE** and **POLLY** are alone.)*

CHARLIE. Well.

POLLY. Well. I think I found the combination of being lover and mother to the same person irresistible.

CHARLIE. I'm sure that's psychologically sound.

POLLY. Did you mean those nice things you said about me?

CHARLIE. Of course. And more.

POLLY. I do like you, you are so observant. But why didn't you say those things to me?

CHARLIE. I did. I directed them at Marc, but I knew they would ricochet.

POLLY. It's true. You are a genius.

(*He smiles.*)

Then you and me, Charlie. Is it by default?

CHARLIE. I should say not. It is the efficacious evolution of events.

POLLY. And, Charlie, you sure you won't hold Marc against me.

CHARLIE. Are you sure you won't hold…

POLLY. Please, don't start listing names. There's no telling how long that would take.

CHARLIE. Well, at least, we have one good thing going for us…Mattresses tell no tales.

(*She laughs.*)

There's a breeze coming in now from the ocean. Would you like to walk along the bluff and watch the birds bathe in the fountain? We can discuss recycling lives.

POLLY. I would love it. As soon as the moving men come so I can dismiss them.

CHARLIE. Then let's make good use of the time.

(*He turns on the music. Dance music they did not dance to before.*)

(*He turns to take her in his arms. But she doesn't move toward him. Instead, her eyes go to his computer.*)

(*He understands immediately what she means…He gets the disc on which he has all the information about the women, drops it in the wastebasket.*)

Ah, yes. Who needs short-term women when there's an open-end one all yours?

(*He reaches for* **POLLY***; they dance as:*)

(*blackout*)

(*curtain*)

COSTUMES

ACT I, Scene One

GWEN: Huge bathtowel
Casual beach clothes Sandals or slipons

CHARLIE: Pajamas
Running suit
Running shoes or loafers
Helmet for moped ride

POLLY: Dowdy dress, dull color
Black, ordinary shoes
Few inexpensive, jewelry pieces Helmet for moped
ride

ELAINE: Latest fashion, upscale
Pants suit
Expensive jewelry: Wrist watch,
Necklace, earrings, wedding ring
Pointed shoes

ROBERT: Business suit
White shirt
Conservative tie
Lace up shoes

ACT I, Scene Two

CHARLIE: Cotton slacks
Loose colorful shirt Loafers
Dark-framed glasses

POLLY: Colorful beach attire/sweater

MARC: Airline pilot's uniform

ACT I, Scene Two

CHARLIE: Cook's hat.
Smock covering most of hisclothes
Tuxedo
Black tie
Crisp whiteshirt
French cuffs
Black shoes
Silver wrist watch

ELAINE: Latest fashion. Upscale
If pants suit,different than in Act I/ Scene 2
Pointed shoes/ different color than earlier
Expensive jewelry

ROBERT:	Second business suit
	White shirt
	Conservative tie/ different than earlier

HARRIET:	Light topcoat.
	Trashy lingerie/ black and red lace
	Garters/ etc.

| POLLY: | Gorgeous, glittering gown |
| | Stylish jewelry |

| MARC: | Airline pilot's uniform |

ACT II, Scene One

| CHARLIE: | Casual beach attire |
| | No shoes/ stocking feet |

| ELAINE: | Latest fashion. Upscale Different than earlier |
| | Pointed shoes/ different color |

POLLY:	Hawaiian skirt and top Lei
MARC:	Hawaiian shirt
	Slacks

ACT II, Scene Two

| CHARLIE: | Casual beach attire |

| GWEN: | Casual beach attire |

| HARRIET: | Casual beach attire |

| ROBERT: | First business suit |
| | White shirt/ open at collar |

ACT II, Scene Three

ELAINE:	Latest fashion. Upscale
	Different than in previous scenes Pointed shoes,
	different color

CHARLIE:	Robe
	Cotton pants/bright shirt
	Loafers
ROBERT:	Sport coat
	Contrasting slacks
	Bright shirt/ open at collar
POLLY:	Simple: dress
	Simple jewelry
MARC:	Airplane pilot's uniform

PROPERTIES

ACT I, Scene One
Thick colored candle, burnt down
Empty champagne bottle
Ice bucket
Carry-all (Saks Fifth Ave.)
Telephone. Answering machine
Dishes. Pots.
Six old fashioned man's white shirts
List. Of things Elaine has to do
Thermometer
Petitions
Coin
Towel
Addressograph machine
Envelopes, legal size
Fax machine, fax message
Computer, disc
Trash
Attaché case
Cordless phone
Wrench
Picture album
String bag
2 Helmets for moped ride
Moped (if seen)

ACT I, Scene Two
Man's dark-framed eyeglasses
Bouquet of flowers
Makings for tea
Book with dust cover

ACT I, Scene Three
Table set, romantic tone
Candles
Bouquet of flowers
Ice bucket, towel
Large letters on wall reading "Happy Birthday"
Pots and pans
Champagne/ the Flower bottle
Champagne glasses
Attache case

ACT II, Scene One
Binoculars
Attache case
Massage lounge chair, which is in Charlie's place at outset
Massage slippers
Ukelele
Circulars, orange and green
Envelopes, legal size
Wet sponge

ACT II, Scene Two
Attache case

ACT II, Scene Three
Music albums
Attache case
Ice bag
Coin
Cane
Books
Hot water bottle
Huge plant
Disc
Wastebasket

Also by
Lawrence Roman...

Alone Together

Alone Together Again

Make Me a Match

P. S. I Love You

OTHER TITLES AVAILABLE FROM SAMUEL FRENCH

P.S. I LOVE YOU

Lawrence Roman

Full Length, Comedy / 4m, 4f

Geraldine Page originated the lead role on Broadway as the wife of an American foreign service officer, meets a dashing and gallant Frenchman at a fashionable spa abroad. The Frenchman presses his suit, but surprisingly it isn't what you expect at all. He is a jaded gallant, tired of both wife and mistresses, and all he wants of the American wife is the privilege of writing her love letters when they return to their separate addresses. She in turn romanticizes the situation, and everything would be delightfully innocent except that her husband and the Frenchman's wife don't believe in innocense. Capping the ensuing complications is the visit of the American to the Frenchman, armed for the kill. A tintillating notion for a seesaw comedy by the author of *UNDER THE YUM YUM TREE.*

"A smart, light comedy of marriage (with) lively farcial moments."
– New York Daily News

OTHER TITLES AVAILABLE FROM SAMUEL FRENCH

ALONE TOGETHER

Lawrence Roman

Comedy / 4m., 2f / Int.

Remember those wonderful Broadway comedies of the fifties and sixties? This play by the author of *UNDER THE YUM YUM TREE* is firmly in that tradition. *ALONE TOGETHER* delighted audiences on Broadway with Janis Paige and Kevin McCarthy playing a middle aged couple whose children have finally left the nest. They are alone together, but not for long. All three sons come charging back home after experiencing some hard knocks in the real world, and Mom and Dad have quite a time pushing them out again.

"An amiable comedy.... The audience roared with recognition, pleasure and amusement."
– *Gannett Westchester Newspaper*

"Delightfully wise and witty."
– *Hollywood Reporter*

"One of the funniest shows we've seen in ages."
– *Herald News*